Praise for Bonnie Dee & Summer Devon's
Mending Him

"*Mending Him* was like dark chocolate: sweet enough to be a dessert, and bitter enough to do the flavors justice."

~ *Heroes and Heartbreakers*

"I am a big fan of Bonnie Dee and Summer Devon's historicals and *Mending Him* was another really delightful story. Robbie and Charles are such an interesting match and I loved the way things develop between them"

~ *Joyfully Jay*

"A pitch perfect historical romance. I've read a good number of Devon and Dee's books, and it's quite safe to say that *Mending Him...* is their best offering yet."

~ *The Novel Approach*

"This story is a sweet, tender love story that made my heart smile while I read it."

~ *Love Bytes Reviews*

"I recommend it to everyone who enjoys a historical romance, passionate men, and true love overcoming almost impossible obstacles."

~ *Rainbow Book Reviews*

Look for these titles by
Bonnie Dee

Now Available:

Look for these titles by
Summer Devon

Now Available:

Mending Him

Bonnie Dee & Summer Devon

SAMHAIN
PUBLISHING

Samhain Publishing, Ltd.
11821 Mason Montgomery Road, 4B
Cincinnati, OH 45249
www.samhainpublishing.com

Mending Him
Copyright © 2014 by Bonnie Dee & Summer Devon
Print ISBN: 978-1-61922-700-2
Digital ISBN: 978-1-61922-329-5

Editing by Linda Ingmanson
Cover by Lou Harper

First Samhain Publishing, Ltd. electronic publication: September 2014
First Samhain Publishing, Ltd. print publication: September 2015

Dedication

To Loki, Molly, Susie, Zoey, Buttons, Gizmo, and Robin, because we appreciate our furry coworkers who help ground us in reality.

Chapter One

"Cousin Robbie, can you help me with my sash? Mary doesn't tie as good a bow as you." Gemma turned her back so Robbie could reconfigure the broad satin band around her plump waist. He didn't mind. The child was right. He *was* better than her nanny at making a perfect bow.

The little girl had found in him in the library where he was putting the last touches on turning the book-lined space into a welcoming bedroom for an invalid to recover in. With all the dark woodwork, this room would never be anything but gloomy, but he'd brought in some flowers and colorful paisley scarves draped across several surfaces to at least try to lift their guest's spirits.

Robbie bent to examine the pale rose ribbon that straggled down from Gemma's waist. To make a greater contrast to the pink organdy gown, the ribbon should be a bright apple green. His mouth watered at the thought of something bold with those luscious colors. But not on a child. Perhaps a large room. A painting, yes, he could see a painting with those complementary colors blazing with no apology across a landscape.

"Aren't you done yet?"

He fluffed out the butterfly wings and smoothed the trailing ribbons before giving her a pat on the back. "There. I couldn't convince you to perhaps read a book?" he asked. It was something of a private joke between them.

"But my story is boring, and the puppies are so darling," she protested. "Anyway, what does it matter what I look like? No one will even notice if I'm not there."

"You must be present to greet your Cousin Charles. It's the polite thing to do."

Gemma sighed deeply, as if "the polite thing" were akin to being placed on the rack. Robbie smiled. Perhaps she was right. He wasn't looking forward to a strained and awkward meeting with the new addition to their household. Another relative, like himself, forced to rely on the kindness of the Chester family.

"Why does he have to come and stay here?" Gemma whined. "Why do we have a cousin we've never even met?"

"Your Cousin Charles is from the north. He lives very far away, which is why he's never been to visit before. But he is your father's cousin, and so a second cousin to you. He's family, and when family is in trouble, we help them out."

"I suppose so." Gemma brightened. "Like you. Right, Robbie? You're like our brother, except not."

"That's right." He smiled and stroked the springy red-gold curls that framed the girl's round face.

"Did his parents have a steamboat blow up under their very feet as well?"

Robbie had told her the truth of his parents' death. He didn't believe in veiling reality with talk of God calling them home, as his Aunt Lenore would've told her daughter. He hadn't counted on the relish small children took from dreadful stories.

"Yes, I believe he's alone in the world." Or Mr. Charles Worthington wouldn't be forced to rely on his cousin for aid during his time of crisis.

"Do you miss your parents very much?" Gemma asked. This was another part of her usual list of questions.

"Yes. I miss them very much." Thanks in part to time and to Gemma's frequent questions, the pain had leached from the memory. Yet they remained vivid: the numbing shock of the initial aftermath of the accident, as if he himself had been submerged in that icy water, followed by intense pain in the weeks and months that followed. Not only had he lost his parents but his home as well.

"But you came to live with us, and then everything was fine," Gemma concluded.

He leaned to kiss the top of her head. "Yes, of course. Everything was fine."

The standard litany over, she could relax. She smiled and picked up her ball from the floor, but before she left the room, she had one more question, a new one she hadn't asked before.

"You'll always be here. Right, Robbie?"

He smiled. Her childish trust was touching, and he didn't want to disappoint her, but he couldn't spend the rest of his life clattering around the Chester estate. Even with his disability, surely he could do something more with his life.

"I'll be here when you need me," he offered.

Gemma grinned and clattered off to find the puppies in their kennel by the stable. He had no illusions she'd sit quietly and look at a picture book.

Robbie decided it was time to retire to his room and see about his own appearance. A clean collar and cuffs and a different waistcoat would present a better appearance to the stranger who would be arriving in less than an hour.

Charles Worthington. Uncle Phillip's cousin. Family rallied when one of their own was in need, and it sounded as if Worthington was in desperate straits. The man had been in a carriage accident that left him with one cracked and one badly broken leg. His money had run out, and he could no longer pay servants to care for him. He'd had no choice but to visit his

11

country relatives, the Chesters, for a prolonged stay while he healed.

Robbie freshened up at his wash basin, slicked down his brown hair and replaced both collar and cuffs on his blue shirt. He regarded his reflection in the mirror. Presentable and forgettable as always. That was fine with him. Blending into the wallpaper could prove useful at times, when people said more than they intended to in his presence.

When he was freshened, Robbie took a book and went to sit with it out in the garden for a rare break from the work he did for his uncle. On such a fine, windy day, he would've preferred to take a walk on the heath, but it was important to Uncle Phillip that the entire family be present for his cousin's arrival, an undivided unit welcoming Charles into their home.

At any rate, his hip was aching quite a lot today. Better that he didn't hike too far and then have to turn around and hobble his way home. Sometimes his intentions outreached his abilities, and he was forced to rely more on his cane. Robbie limped downstairs, the foot on his shorter leg hitting each step with a thump. Having a paralyzing fever as a child had permanently altered his gait. He'd lived with a withered leg for most of his life and rarely thought about it, except when meeting new people. Their curious or pitying glances were a trial he preferred to avoid when possible.

He brushed fallen crab apples from the wrought iron bench beneath the small fruit tree and dropped onto the bench with a small grunt. What a pleasure to spend some time studying Da Vinci's drawings in the precious art book he'd received as a present from his aunt last Christmas. But even the master's artwork couldn't hold his attention today. His mind kept drifting to the impending arrival of the new houseguest.

What would Charles Worthington be like? Perhaps an ally, someone with whom he could converse or maybe challenge in a game of chess? Robbie's younger cousins, ten-year-old Bertie and seven-year-old Gemma, were dear to him, but they were hardly companions with whom he might share adult conversation. As for Cousin Samuel, although he was nearer to Robbie in age, they would never be close friends. The more Robbie worked with Uncle Phillip on the estate, the more distant Samuel became. Ever since he'd gone to university, he'd become nearly antagonistic to Robbie, who was at a loss as to how to remedy the situation or repair their relationship. Samuel was taking a tour of Europe after his graduation, and perhaps he'd return to the hall feeling friendlier toward Robbie.

Robbie heard the cart from the train station coming up the gravel drive. His pulse quickened as he rose and walked around to the front of the house to greet the new addition to the household.

The servants didn't line up to be greeted and inspected. This was not a visit by a lord of the estate, merely the arrival of an impoverished relation. But Aunt Lenore had the children assembled on the lawn, *"to provide a welcoming atmosphere."* The day was so pleasant that Gemma and Bertie weren't complaining, though Bertie kept thumping the ground with a croquet mallet he'd found and Gemma picked a ruffle on her pinafore.

The sound of the approaching cart reached the lawn, and the children stopped chasing each other around the grass to watch the drive expectantly.

A keening voice sang in time with the clop of the pony's hoofbeats.

"Good heavens," Aunt Lenore hissed, then in a louder voice, "Mary, take the children inside. Now, please. Yes, I mean it, Bertie. I think perhaps we shan't have a formal greeting for Cousin Charles after all."

Robbie bit his lower lip rather than break into laughter—his aunt's agitation was too evident. She turned to her husband. "Is...is that some sort of drinking song?"

"Hm. I think, yes. Perhaps you might go inside as well, my dear." They fell silent long enough that another bawdy verse drifted up to them. In a grim voice, Phillip continued, "I suspect my cousin will not be in a fit state to be in the company of ladies."

The cart rounded the corner and came into view rolling and bumping up the drive.

And now Robbie realized that a low buzzing accompanied the loud tenor. Mr. Forrester, the driver, must have noticed the group gathered by the gravel drive, for the buzzing stopped at once. Mr. Forrester, one of the most silent and grim men Robbie knew, had been singing.

This was a day of mind-boggling surprises.

Uncle Phillip muttered, "Why on earth is he sitting up with the driver? The pony cart seats are an easy, low step up. That was the confounded point of sending it for him."

The open cart was full of bags and a strange contraption of wheels.

The ginger-haired man seated next to Forrester on the cart wore a rumpled dark suit. He lightly thumped the driver's shoulder with his fist. "Carry on, carry on, my good man. We are nearly to the point of no return, but we are not there yet. We remain free and wandering fools for the next several seconds at least." The passenger waved his hand as if conducting a huge orchestra. He saw the group by the entrance to Chester Hall, gave a cry of "View halloo," and launched back into song, something about the lass who could ne'er say no.

Robbie had never heard such a song in his life. Amusement and annoyance and something like anticipation washed over him in competing waves. Such joyful, obscene nonsense.

"Oh no." His aunt still stood next to him. Her hand covered her mouth. "What is he singing?"

Less than fifty feet for the cart to travel.

It would be up to him to escort her inside, and sure enough, Uncle Phillip said, rather sharply, "Robbie. Would you kindly take your aunt indoors?"

Of course that was his role. He nodded, yet he felt a strange reluctance to miss a moment of this grand entrance.

Robbie gave her shoulders a gentle squeeze. "Come along, Aunt Lenore. We shall go speak to Mrs. Jackson about dinner."

"I think she need not rush the meal. Indeed, I think a good lie-down is in order," she added.

He wondered if she meant for herself or for the yodeling man seated on the pony trap. "He has a good voice," he said absently.

"But *such* a song, Robbie." She sounded near tears. "My children. You, my dear boy. It is not at all the thing."

He wanted to protest that at twenty-three he was hardly a child, but he only kissed her cheek. "It will be fine. He is inebriated, and the children couldn't understand the words of the song."

In fact, Charles Worthington enunciated extremely well for a drunkard, but soothing Aunt Lenore must be Robbie's first concern.

"Perhaps he dislikes travel," he added.

Another loud warbling verse reached them. This one contained language—obviously obscene words—Robbie didn't know. He felt poorly educated.

She clutched his arm. "Do you suppose he could be violent? I have heard that some men in their cups can cause great harm. Do go help your uncle cope with him. There's a good boy." She'd occasionally asked him to take over the care of her fractious offspring in just such a manner. He didn't bother to point out a limping and slightly built man would present no sort of threat to anyone bent on violence. Robbie could soothe a child in a tantrum, but he was less certain about his ability to cope with a caroling sot.

Yet he had to hide a smile, for he felt exhilaration at the notion of encountering the drunken singer.

"Of course." He gently removed her hand from his jacket and gave it a squeeze.

"Come find me as soon as you get that man into his room." She paused and pressed her lips tight. "I spent hours rearranging the library so he might be able to wheel his Bath chair into it and never encounter stairs. I shouldn't want a man like that driving anything, not even a chair, especially not in the house." She reddened as if voicing her disapproval showed too much emotion. "But go, do. And see what might be done."

Outside, Uncle Phillip stood scowling, his arms folded, watching Forrester wrestle with a bulky green and wood and bronze contraption that had been wedged into the passenger compartment. A chair.

"Here now, don't break m'leg again, my good Forrester," Worthington warbled, still singing. "I have no legs but those. And crutches," he added in a regular voice. He leaned over and seemed to grope along the back of the seat.

He straightened, pulling the sticks out from under something. Yanking hard, he seemed about to overset himself.

Uncle Phillip made a disgusted noise and turned his back.

Forrester, wrestling with the chair, didn't notice.

Robbie limped quickly toward the carriage. For a moment, he took in the redheaded man's features—the high-bridged hatchet of a nose that made an emphatic statement, a pair of brown eyes which sparkled in the sunlight, a wide mouth bracketed by deep grooves. He looked like a man who made it his business to smile and laugh often, and just looking at him made Robbie start to smile too.

Worthington gave another, stronger pull at the crutches tucked behind the seat, and that proved too much.

Robbie reached up as if he'd be able to stop the inevitable fall. He didn't of course.

"Oh *bugger* this," Worthington said and slowly toppled over the armrest and fell on top of Robbie.

Robbie landed hard on the gravel, the weight of the long-limbed man crushing him down. He heard something in his shoulder click and was instantly filled with pain.

Worthington yelped. "Damnation! I've killed you. Are you hurt?"

Robbie wiggled and shouted, ready to bite the idiot if he didn't get that weight off his shoulder, but the man on top of him didn't stand up. Oh, that's right, Robbie finally recalled. He couldn't.

Worthington dragged his great weight off by crawling, then settled with a rattle and crunch on the gravel next to Robbie.

"'S your shoulder, boy. I hurt your shoulder," Worthington said, sounding as if he was about to burst into tears. "I didn't mean to."

"No of course you didn't," gasped Robbie. He closed his eyes and wondered if he might use an awful word to express his own vile pain.

"Here, now, wait a moment. Wait now! I have it! I do. You, my own Forrester." The drunk man's shouts seemed to pierce Robbie's already aching head. "You hold his body. Just there. Hold him tight. And I'll just give a bit of a pull. Not a yank, no indeed."

"What the devil do you think you are doing?" Uncle Phillip came forward and entered the fray.

"His shoulder. Poor mite's got it dissslocolated. Located. I did that, sorry, sorry. I didn't mean to, I assure you. Lost my balance. Mr. Forrester, my man. Yes. Hold him still. That's the way."

Forrester seemed to be taking orders from the man who reeked of brandy, for large arms in gray homespun suddenly wrapped around Robbie's body.

"That's it," the drunken fool cheered. "That's the way." He grabbed Robbie's arm and, ignoring both Robbie's cry of pain and Uncle Phillip's shouts, pulled up and out and...

Click. The agony ceased.

Robbie could breathe again. Forrester let go of him a bit too soon, and he landed on his arse, but the pain had ended.

Worthington, also on his bottom on the gravel, beamed at him. "All better, my boy? Here, now, you're not a boy, though, are you? You are a man. With a relocated shoulder. Indeed." He sounded absolutely delighted. "But don't use that arm too much, all right? Alllll right. Maybe even a sling. Yes. That's the very ticket. Get my friend Mr. Forrester to get you a sling."

Robbie took his time standing up. He grabbed hold of the carriage with his good arm to haul himself along.

Uncle Phillip suddenly appeared to help, but by then, Robbie had regained his feet and had his cane again.

Worthington smiled up at them both, a glorious white-toothed broad grin. He waved at Phillip. "So you must be my cousin Phillip! It has been a great many years. And this is your boy, young Bertie, or was it Samuel? Not yours, I think, for isn't he too old? But never mind. Never mind. I say, I didn't mean to injure your sons the moment I arrived."

"Cousin Charles, you are the worse for drink," Phillip said coolly.

"Why do you think they call it the worse?" Worthington turned to Robbie and asked conversationally, almost sounding sober. "I'd say it was the better. Except for you, poor Bertie. I landed on you because, yes, I am drunk." His grin reappeared, then vanished. "But it isn't merely that I imbibed too freely. I also am used to bracing myself just so with my feet. I raced in curricles and braced with my feet. You know? And I can't. No indeed, I cannot. And so I fell. Boom. On top of you, poor, poor Bertie."

"I am Robert."

"Don't like to be called Bertie, then?"

Forrester had gotten the behemoth of a chair out of the carriage.

"Ah, my miserable steed awaits," Charles said. "Lend me a hand, Bertie?"

"I am Robbie Grayson, Mrs. Chester's nephew." He wondered why it was so important that this singing drunken man know who he was. He reached down to help haul up Charles.

"No, oh no! We forgot your arm." He rolled his eyes, which were brown and large and remarkably clear. "Forget my own name next. You never mind. Forgive me. Cousin Phillip and my beloved Forrester, I shall have to beg for your help. Haul me onto the cursed chair, please. I might manage with those sticks, my crutches, but another time when the world is less spinning and dipping."

"Drunk," Uncle Phillip muttered.

"We can all agree that is my condition," Charles said happily. "And I should apologize for appearing in such a state, but you see, I can't walk." As he settled into the chair, he hiccupped gently. "I drink to forget," he said and then gave a hoot of laughter. "And then when I forget too much, I fall right over, boom, on poor unsuspecting boys. I mean men. Not boys, men, who are simply coming to my aid. Such a punishment for such chivalry, Bertie."

"I am Rob—"

"Oh yes. I recall, and furthermore, I shall never again forget that you are Robbie, like our own dear Rabbie Burns. Robbie. I know you're Robbie. Robbie, Robbie..." He sang out the name over and over. And then he started reciting a strange version of Burns's poetry in that thick, drunk, magnificent voice. "A wee sleekit timorous Robbie mouse."

Robbie, arm aching and head a little thick, fully aware that his Uncle Phillip was in a foul temper, still found himself smiling at the strange new guest.

"Perhaps that's enough of a poetry recitation for now, Mr. Worthington. I'll show him to his room, Uncle Phillip." Robbie glanced at the big-eyed footman, Stewart, who was helping Forrester unload the luggage from the cart. Oh, they'd be talking below-stairs about this grand entrance for months to come.

"Very well. And I'll make certain your aunt isn't too overcome." Phillip glowered at his drunken cousin. "This will not do at all, Charles, if you intend to stay here. I have opened my home to you and am glad to do so, but such outrageous behavior is unacceptable."

"Yes, sir." The chastened reply was punctuated by a loud hiccup that somewhat detracted from any sense of earnestness.

Robbie ducked his head to hide his face while he struggled to fend off inappropriate laughter. He couldn't push the chair one-handed, so Stewart took on that task, hard work over the lawn. Two footmen and Forrester had to haul the invalid up the several stairs into the house.

Robbie led the way to the library where Worthington was to be installed for the duration of his recovery. "I'm sure you'll find this much more comfortable than any of the bedrooms on the second floor. It can get a bit cold and drafty upstairs." He spoke to cover the sudden silence of the sodden Charles, who, it appeared, might have passed out. At any rate, his chin rested on his chest and his hands were slack in his lap.

"Thank you, Stewart," Robbie said. "Will you be needing additional aid in dressing or getting in and out of bed, Mr. Worthington? I'm sure Stewart could help with anything you might need."

"Happy to, sir," the footman piped up, probably hoping this might be a stepping stone to acting as a gentleman's gentleman someday.

Worthington lifted his head and squinted. "No. I'm able to get in and out of the chair and hobble around a bit by myself—when I'm not in my cups. Dashed foolish way to arrive on my cousin's doorstep, cap in hand and squiffed."

Robbie lowered himself so his gaze was level with Worthington's. "You mustn't feel that way, you know, as if you had come begging. Uncle Phillip and Aunt Lenore are happy to have you. Truly. We all are. For as long as you should need or want to stay. You'll find this is a comfortable home with a loving family. *Your* family, after all. So don't hesitate to ask for anything you need."

There. He'd done his part, hopefully made poor drunken Charles feel a little more welcome. He felt odd making the speech he knew wasn't really his place to give, but the man needed some sort of reassurance.

Robbie awkwardly squatted in a cantilevered stance, fighting to keep his balance. His gaze locked with Worthington's, and the man's eyes appeared rather less bleary and unfocused. He frowned as he stared back at Robbie with eyes as brown as a polished teak desk. So dark and intent that Robbie dropped his gaze lest the other man see his sudden flare of attraction.

"Thank you for that, Bertie," Worthington said in a deep voice that scraped across Robbie's nerves like gravel. "Or, no, damn. Cousin Robert, I should call you."

"No. Not cousin. I am Lenore's nephew," Robbie reminded him. "And you are Phillip's cousin. So we are no real relations at all, except perhaps by marriage." Again he felt the need to stress that. But why? What did it matter if Charles Worthington lumped him together with the rest of his second cousins in his mind?

"Right," Worthington said in the overly emphatic tone drunks used. "I do appreciate your kindness, Robert, but I don't need or want a family looking after me as if I were a child. What I *need* is to regain the use of my legs and be able to stand on my own again. I need to be a man and not a charity case."

"Of course. I understand." Robbie rose stiffly to his feet, doing his damnedest not to wobble. "Very well, then, Mr. Worthington. I shall see you at dinner I suppose. Have a nice rest and see if you can't collect yourself by then."

Charity case. Just like Robbie Grayson. He turned and walked out of the room with his back as erect as he could make it. Those scornful words might have been a punch in the gut, and the ache in his shoulder was nothing in comparison.

Chapter Two

Damn his foolish drunken tongue. Charles suddenly felt as sober as he'd been before the start of this long day's journey to hell and the flask of whisky he'd sipped along the way. He'd just insulted poor, lame Cousin Robbie, who might have been a good ally to have here.

"Not a cousin," he reminded himself aloud. "And I do remember what Phillip told me about him now."

He hadn't really paid close attention to the details of the Chester family. He supposed he hadn't really wanted to know, as thinking of the family as individual people would make them a reality. And he'd wanted to avoid truth as often as possible and for as long as he could.

Reality meant facing the fact that all of his money was gone. He'd had to let go his staff first, then the paintings and family heirlooms, then the furniture, sold by McNair, who'd turned into the final remaining surly retainer. McNair took a percentage in lieu of back wages. At last the empty house went on the market. Only when he teetered on the edge of relying on some charitable institution did Charles ask his Cousin Phillip for help. He simply couldn't take care of himself, and he was out of options. The niggling fear that he might never recover his mobility, or his ability to earn for himself, hovered at the edge of his consciousness all the time. Fear, like little white larvae wiggling in rotten fruit.

He'd lied to that nice cripple, Robbie, telling him he didn't need the footman's help. The truth was Charles couldn't hobble around at all. He might possibly be able to heave himself from the chair onto the bed, but even that was doubtful. And he certainly couldn't unpack his luggage or change his clothes.

McNair. How he missed the old sod who'd acted as his valet for most of his adult life. The man used to drive Charles insane with his attention to detail, but he'd give anything to have him back now. And the money. God, how he missed having money with which he could hire people to perform the tasks he needed until he was on his feet again.

But since he was being honest with himself at last, the money had been depleting long before too many years of unpaid bills drained him dry, and then with the illness, he had no way to fight the creditors or find a way to make income. He'd lived high and fast for too long on the thin remnants of his family fortune and was lucky to have had enough to pay for the physicians he'd needed.

Charles saw his life laid out behind him—a wastrel spending money as if it would regenerate, and his dreary future spread before him—locked in a wheelchair and forced to rely on charity at least for the near future, and who knew if he would ever truly recover. He squeezed his eyes tightly shut to keep back the tears that threatened to ooze out yet again. Christ, he'd cried more over the past month than he had in his entire life.

You have no one to blame but yourself. The cool yet loving voice was one he ascribed to his mother, though in reality he'd never known the woman. She'd died when he was only six months old, but the little whispering voice of conscience that haunted him when he was doing wrong things always sounded like a woman. That was what a mother was for, wasn't it? To keep one on the straight and narrow.

Too bad he hadn't heeded those imaginary warnings, or he wouldn't be in the mess he was today. If he'd bothered to work at something, anything. If he'd learned to save and judiciously invest, instead of toss money down the black hole of a gaming table... If he'd not spent so much on beautiful clothes and wine... If only... What stupid and annoying words they were.

"Pouting does not become you, Charles." He quoted one very dear man he'd had had the pleasure to know for the better part of a year, Paul Martin. What was Paul doing right this second? If Charles were to send him a telegram, would he respond? Probably not. That particular friendship had ended on less than amicable terms.

Come to think of it, most of his very special friendships had. He was built for brief encounters rather than long relationships. And now, without any money to ease the way, he would be hard pressed to manage any dalliances at all. What was life going to be like here in this backwater with nothing to do except recover his ability to walk? He had no one to talk to, although that Robbie didn't seem like a bad sort. At the very least, he might find a chess partner in him.

Charles pushed the big wheels on either side of him with all his strength and was able to roll closer to the bed. He braced his hands on the support for the arms. One, two, three, and he lifted his body up on arms that shook from the effort. Sweat rolled down his face, and shooting pains radiated from his broken legs like flashes of lightning. He supposed he should be grateful there *was* pain, since his spinal cord or some other even more necessary part of him could been damaged in the accident. As for those symptoms that had begun *before* the accident, the odd tingling and loss of control in his muscles which had, in fact, led to the crash, they were passing slowly. Most days he almost felt normal again.

Now, up on his feet. Charles balanced for two whole seconds before falling across the narrow bed. The frame groaned under his weight and the soft mattress swallowed him. Too soft. He preferred a harder bed, but then beggars couldn't be choosers. Charles laughed into the coverlet that nearly smothered him. A beggar. He was little more than that now.

He lay half on and half off the bed, helpless as an infant, unable to even remove his tight shoes or strip off the coat that bound him like a straitjacket. Unable to make it to the water closet and relieve himself—if they even had modern facilities in this old place, and damn, he had to piss like a horse after all he'd drunk. He truly had reached bottom. For a man who'd never experienced hopelessness or despair in his life, it was quite a shock to discover the debilitating power of such feelings.

"No pouting, Charles," he reminded himself again. "It will make lines on your handsome face." Foolish, stupid man. He'd been so focused on fashionable clothing and the beautiful things money could buy, on winning at cards and fun to be had and places to see. But when all those things were stripped away, who was he underneath? A figure molded from ash and air.

He flopped onto his back and stared at the ceiling, while time crawled or perhaps sped by. He wasn't sure which, for the bed was spinning along with his brain, and time was immeasurable. To stop the nauseating motion, he stared at an orange water stain scrawled across the ceiling like cryptic writing. If he could read the message, what would it say, something intriguing or earth shaking? No. Not in this staid and unpretentious house. No secret assignations had taken place on this narrow bed. No epic love story unfolded or unrequited passion consummated at last beneath such a humdrum ceiling.

Charles examined the stain and wished again that he hadn't sent that footman away so quickly. Or that non-cousin, Robbie Grayson. There was a light of intelligence in his sympathetic eyes, a character who might be interesting to know. Besides, Charles could've asked him questions about what life was like here at the Chester house. How did Robbie feel about the Chester family and his place in it? He'd lived here since boyhood, as Charles now recalled. So, did wee Robbie with the lame leg feel a part of the family or permanently outside of it?

Charles's stomach churned, and his need to piss became painful. He must find a chamber pot. Muzzy-headed, but still uncomfortably aware that most of his body seemed composed of a bottomless well of piss and self-pity, he at last managed to drag himself back off the bed. No chamber pot lay under the bed.

He looked about the room, a library built by a man who wanted to impress visitors with his wealth. Charles had had such a room on the second story of his London house.

Yes, there was standard dark paneling and the opulent Sienna marble fireplace and mantel. He craned his neck and saw that through the door was another room that was likely a billiard room. Not a water closet, more's the pity.

He spotted a tall brass vase full of a strange arrangement of dried and glass flowers, and he set off across the polished parquet floor, using a motion more like swimming than crawling. Really, one might congratulate oneself for remembering to pull out the arrangement before using the vase.

He finished relieving himself, carefully replaced the vase on the floor and, with familiar despair, realized the bed was too far away. He could not drag himself back.

Even rolling onto his side was more than he could manage, so he pitched forward, sprawled on his stomach, face pressed against the rough wool of a Persian carpet.

He passed out.

He awoke minutes later—or perhaps it was hours—with the horrible knowledge that he was going to be sick. He could barely summon the strength to heave. This is the moment, he thought as he lay too near the stinking vomit. *This is when I change or die.*

"Oh good Christ. What a mess." An unfamiliar male voice spoke with utter disgust. A servant, perhaps the footman who'd helped him in.

Charles agreed with the evaluation, but he wouldn't turn his head or open his eyes. Maybe if he concentrated, he could will himself to die.

"Hold thou my sword-hilts, whilst I run on it," he muttered into the rug.

"That would create an even greater mess," said another very quiet, gently amused voice near his head. "You would fall upon your sword and leave some poor servant to clean up the mess."

The non-cousin, Robbie Grayson.

A rustle of cloth and a thump. In a louder voice, Grayson said, "Never mind, leave the bucket here, and I shall take care of it." There was a swish of water and the thump of some sort of wooden bucket.

Was the man ever not cheerful?

"It's disgusting. Showing up like a drunkard and—good lord, what has he done with Mrs. Chester's vase? Has he...? Is that vomit?" A woman's voice, low and quiet. Another servant. Apparently the servants didn't mind complaining in front of Robbie Grayson.

Grayson interrupted, still calm. "I'll attend to it. Please do take the vase with you, Mrs. Jackson. Clean it out and return it, and I'll put the arrangement back together."

"Of course, Master Robbie," she said. "I'll fetch another pail. Best to use cold water in these cases. The smell."

"So I remember from Gemma's illness," Robbie said. "I have an iron stomach, and I'm aware you don't."

"You are an angel. I'd send one of the girls, but they don't need to see this...this sort of thing."

"No indeed. Thank you, Mrs. Jackson. Stewart, please wait outside. I'll call if I need you."

The door closed softly. For a long moment, Charles thought he was alone. Then he heard the soft inhalation of a man stifling a sigh or a yawn. Which was it? And why was Robert Grayson sent to do this sort of task?

He almost wished they'd sent Forrester. For some reason, he'd hoped to make a good impression on Grayson. Too late for that now. Ah well, he'd be the drunken sot who puked on the good library carpet and pissed in the vase.

"I know you're awake, Mr. Worthington. Shall we bend to the task before us?"

Charles made a small protesting noise.

"We have three arms and one useful leg between us, so I think we shall manage. Don't you?" The soft thump and drag of the man's halting step told Charles he moved about the room again.

"We have a simple goal—to undress you, clean you up a bit and shovel you into the bed once more."

"You sound appallingly cheerful."

"Yes, I have been accused of that offense before." Robbie's smile was obvious in his voice. "Can you sit up?"

Charles rolled onto his side and then wished he hadn't. "God, I am mortified, Mr. Grayson. I feel... Oh no..."

Robbie was there at once with some sort of a container, a bucket.

When he was done, Charles groaned and wiped his mouth with his sleeve. "I am sorrier than I can express. I wish I knew what I could do, what I ought..." He wasn't sure how he could finish that sentence without sounding even more pitiful.

"Ah, but I know what you ought to do."

Tell me. Please. Tell me how to recover my legs and my dignity.

"You should rinse out the taste," Robbie said, calm as ever.

Charles opened his dry, grainy eyes to see a glass of water, held by a hand with square, close-cut nails. Did Robbie Grayson bite his nails?

"Thank you." He wanted to say more but wasn't sure he trusted his voice. He took the glass.

"Spit there." Robbie pointed at the bucket.

He obeyed, then drank some of the cool, sweet water.

"Here you go." Robbie handed him a cloth that had been dipped in water and something that smelled of mint.

The rotten taste in his mouth banished, the cool cloth on his nape—gradually Charles could feel something other than abject misery. The embarrassment remained, despite Robbie's easy manner.

Robbie squatted near him, cleaning the rug. He rose carefully and carried the tin buckets to the door.

Charles dragged himself up to sit, propped against the cabinet where the vase had been.

"You are very kind," he said as he concentrated on unbuttoning his waistcoat with trembling fingers.

"Not at all," said Robbie. "Hardly worth mentioning."

Charles knew otherwise. Robbie Grayson could have been scornful or appalled or simply left him to the servants, but he had come in and taken charge and treated Charles with simple friendliness.

Charles glanced over at him. Robbie stood in only his shirtsleeves and some poorly tailored trousers. He'd hooked his thumbs in the braces and leaned a hip against a low bookshelf, the picture of a gentleman at leisure.

"Let me know if you require my aid," he said when their eyes met. He looked away; Charles didn't. Enough alcohol still swirled through his system that he allowed himself a thorough perusal.

Grayson's shoulders weren't broad, but he was pleasingly proportioned, and the lines of muscle in his forearms demonstrated hidden strength, Charles fancied. The dark hair on Robbie's arms showed him to be an adult male, not the youth he seemed at first.

Grayson straightened and shuffled near, reaching down to the more-or-less clean, damp spot on the carpet. He grimaced.

"That shoulder is causing you pain." Charles was not used to feeling shame, and he wasn't relishing the weight of it as he recalled how the man's shoulder had been hurt from Charles toppling onto him like some great oaf.

"It's much better." Grayson straightened. "I apologize for not being properly dressed. I was getting ready for bed when I decided someone ought to check on you. I believe I might have heard a thump?"

He'd been getting ready for bed? Charles noticed now the slits of light between the heavy library curtains had vanished. Now the only sources of light were two lamps on the desk that had been shoved into a corner to make room for the cot.

Had Grayson lit them?

Charles had lost hours, and dinnertime as well, which was a pity because his now-empty stomach had begun to grumble.

He awkwardly folded the waistcoat, set it on the floor next to him and began unbuttoning his shirt.

Robbie straightened and looked away. "I'd offer to help, but I think I'd be more likely to get in your way."

Charles would love to drawl something about how he wouldn't mind at all if his dear new friend Robbie got in his way. But, of course, he would not. Although he swore he felt a glimmer of...something simmering in the air between them, it was more likely his hopeful sot's imagination. He would never risk trying to seduce the one man who'd treated him kindly and possibly end up driving him off.

Of course, that driver, Forrester had also been quite kind, sharing the last of his whisky. Charles pulled off his shirt, considering that one change in his new existence that seemed rather freeing. He wasn't used to thinking of servants as any sort of companion. In the past, he wouldn't even talk about personal things with someone like McNair. He'd certainly never noticed the in-between people, men like Robbie, who was not a servant yet appeared to act like a butler or major domo in this house.

"I'm eternally grateful to you, Mr. Grayson." Charles met the translucent gray-green eyes, which seemed to grow sharper even as they examined him.

"You're feeling more the thing? Less dreadful?" Robbie said.

Charles nodded. If he could imagine touching that caring face, drawing it close for a kiss or two, he definitely felt more like himself. "I've rallied, thanks to you."

Robbie laid his hands on Charles's shoulders and carefully squatted. Those hands were large for his slender size and obviously strong. Charles examined them. Definitely bitten nails. His gaze traveled again to the bit of hair that showed at the top of Robbie's unbuttoned shirt. Charles raised his eyes and met the cool gaze. They remained locked together that way for a powerful few moments. Suddenly, the slight Robbie seemed less inconsequential. Charles raised his own hand, intending to cover the warm, strong grip on his shoulder.

"I shall not tell my aunt and uncle about this evening, but the servants know and will likely complain," Robbie whispered, which showed he believed servants to be listening. "This family is not liberal in its views. There is little tolerance for anything unconventional." He paused, then added, "Such as overindulgence in drink."

Charles's hand froze. He lowered it. There was dark warning in those words. Not a threat, of course, but something hard as steel. A message which curbed his budding desire and let him know in unequivocal terms that there was no place for it to take root and grow.

Charles swallowed his thousandth apology and only said, "Ah."

Robbie squeezed both shoulders once, fast, then released his grip. "I needed to warn you." He lurched awkwardly to his feet. Charles reached out to steady him.

"Oh no, I'm quite used to my own clumsiness." The light, pleasant tone had returned to his voice. "I'll remain here and wait until I know you'll be all right."

A light scratch came at the door.

Stewart entered, carrying two empty containers. One was the vase, which he put on the cabinet. The other was a flowered chamber pot.

Robbie nodded, and the footman slid it under the cot.

"It was entirely our fault for forgetting such an important detail. I hope you will forgive us?" Robbie spoke in a normal voice, instead of the middle-of-the-night hushed tones they'd been employing. He watched Stewart, not Charles.

Nice of him to try to remove the blame that belonged to Charles. "Of course," Charles said.

"Stewart, please help Mr. Worthington back into his bed." Robbie's smile seemed perfunctory. "Good night, Cousin Charles. I hope you feel better." He plunked the ugly flower arrangement back into the urn, then hurried out of the room.

Chapter Three

Ruffled. Like a cat whose fur has been stroked the wrong way. Crackles and pops of static electricity prickled his skin and zipped through his bloodstream. Robbie did not care for the feeling *at all*. Nor had he been prepared for a stab of lust to spear through him when he'd merely gone to offer a helping hand to the newcomer.

When he'd imagined Worthington's arrival, at best he'd hoped to gain a friend, someone to spend an amiable hour with now and again. At worse, he'd feared an arrogant snob who would ignore or talk down to him. He had *not* expected Charles Worthington, with his dark brown eyes so full of pain and his deep voice rumbling in way that upset Robbie's equilibrium.

This would not do, as Aunt Lenore would say.

The flutter of excitement that ricocheted around inside him must be exterminated immediately. He'd succeeded in quashing this sort undesirable attraction before, of course. He'd simply left any room Uncle Phillip's lawyer's assistant entered. That man, slender and meek, barely resembled Worthington, but both had smiles that sparked that same swirling fear in Robbie. He'd easily shed that old infatuation and no longer thought of that assistant's hands or smile except of course, at night or quiet times alone.

He deemed it best to keep his distance from Worthington for a while. Let the man gain his bearings here on his own, and, in the meantime, Robbie might find his footing again too.

By the following morning, despite a restless night's sleep, Robbie felt quite himself again as he faced Bertie over a table laden with kippers, eggs and toast in the family's small breakfast room. Gemma still ate in the nursery with her nanny.

"What do you think of Mr. Worthington?" the other Robert in the family, Bertie, asked. The boy regarded Robbie over a toast triangle with a frown reminiscent of his brother, Samuel. "I heard Stewart say to one of the other footmen that Worthington's a sloppy souse."

"Stewart shouldn't be speaking out of turn about our guest. Mr. Worthington was also tired from his journey."

"Well, I thought he was funny with the singing and everything. I think he seems a jolly fellow." Bertie sat back and bit off a toast corner.

"What are your plans for the day, Master Bert?" Robbie changed the subject from the very subject he'd intended *not* to dwell on. "Off hunting for treasure or practicing piracy, I presume?"

"Highwayman," Bertie replied. "In the woods. With Liam, but not Gemma."

"I'm sure she'd love to play and won't be too happy to be left behind. Would you?"

"No. But she's a girl *and* she's too little. She can't climb trees or do anything useful. She can't be a highwayman."

"Hm." Robbie set down his cup and considered the problem. Gemma would cry her eyes red if Bertie and Liam, the local banker's son, spent an entire day rambling in the woods without her. She'd been devastated when Bert first left for school and mourned his loss like a sad little ghost flitting around the house.

"Maybe she could drive the coach you attack, or act as the sheriff searching the woods for your hideout," Robbie improvised. He well recalled what it was like to be the child who was left alone while stronger, healthier boys went out to play, and he felt a powerful urge to make sure Gemma had all the childish fun she could before she was forced into corsets and long skirts.

He leveled his gaze on Bertie. "Your sister misses you dreadfully when you're away at school. You're here for such a short time between terms, couldn't you give a little attention to her? Take her along with you today once she has finished her lessons with Miss Peters."

Bertie grimaced and swallowed the last of his breakfast. "Oh, all right. I 'spose so."

"Good lad." Robbie smiled at his little cousin and earned a quick grin in return.

At nearly eleven, Bertie could not really be called little anymore, Robbie realized. His babyish roundness was honed away, and the man he would someday be emerged in the strong bones of his face and form. Another straight-backed, blond-haired Chester in Uncle Phillip's mold. Robbie only prayed that the sweet child wouldn't grow to be too much like his arrogant older brother. But already there were changes in Bert's character, a cooler exterior, a harder heart, courtesy of boarding school.

Robbie shrugged off miserable memories of his own school days—a bleak and endless time to be sure—and went to find his uncle.

"Sorry to rise so late, sir." Robbie greeted Phillip as he entered the organized clutter of the office where his uncle and the bailiff sat, discussing estate affairs.

Leaning back in his large leather chair, Uncle Phillip nodded. "That's quite all right. You earned a late rest. I thank you for helping out with my Cousin Charles. His arrival was quite an event. An embarrassment to our family, as I'm sure word of this will spread through the village and beyond. Servants enjoy passing on such tidbits of scandal."

Robbie feared his uncle was right. Gossip always oozed through the county like water from a leaky pipe, and although Worthington's sodden state was not the Chesters' fault, the incident would reflect poorly on the family in the community's eyes. Wagging tongues and narrow-minded rural morality— Robbie had once hoped to experience a broader scope of living in London, but his time there had been quickly aborted due to health issues, so here he remained in his country-mouse life.

Robbie took a seat in the straight back chair across the desk from his uncle, stiffly, for both his leg and shoulder were giving him twinges today. He greeted Mr. Todd, a brawny man from the southern part of the county, whom Robbie had urged his uncle to hire after discovering former bailiff, Mr. Smithers, had embezzled from the estate.

"I thank you again for offering a kind hand to my recalcitrant cousin," Phillip said. "The sooner the man is back on his feet, the better. Since you have such a gentle way with children and the infirm, I hope you will continue to help him to recuperate."

Robbie knew that brisk tone well. Uncle Phillip's "I hope you will" meant "you must".

"Oh. I..." Robbie was at a loss. Uncle Phillip required the exact opposite of keeping distance between himself and the annoying yet alluring Charles Worthington. "That is to say, I have my hands full with helping Mr. Todd with the accounts and implementing all the improvements we've discussed. We still haven't decided if diverting that stream in the McGillis's farm is the wisest—"

"I appreciate all you've done to help put the estate back on track, but Mr. Todd is competent to carry on the work. Of course, you're still very necessary, Robbie. Your bookwork is exemplary and I rely on you for your ideas and innovations. You're a very clever young man."

Uncle Phillip leaned forward in his armchair, the worn leather creaking slightly as he shifted. His long features and golden hair fading to gray gave him a leonine appearance—kindly, wise...and decided. "You have served the family well. All your work here has been appreciated, but I think it's time we take another look at your future. I am not certain if you wanted to again try for another apprenticeship. If not, I have acquaintances who could use a good employee in their offices. It's time for you to begin something new."

There it was. The exact thing he'd longed for, extended on a hand of kindness like a piece of enticing fruit. The trouble was he'd grown too comfortable in this little corner of the world, a place where he knew what was expected of him and where he could be of good use. Living on his own in the city was a frightening, if exciting, proposition.

"That would be... I would greatly appreciate that," he stammered.

"For now, however, I'm afraid I count on you to assist my cousin during his recovery. I would like you to stay until he is entirely better." Uncle Phillip drummed his fingers on his desk and cleared his throat. "We've had word that Samuel will be returning home from France sooner than expected. He will be staying at home now. It his duty to take on many of the responsibilities I've relied on you to perform."

Robbie nodded. He even managed a small smile, although he felt a bit as if he'd been slapped. This was the real reason for his uncle's speech about moving on. He was to be replaced.

He'd realized the time would come when Samuel would take his rightful place as heir, yet he'd enjoyed the sense of being an indispensable right hand to his uncle. It hurt to know he wasn't.

During the many years he'd lived with the Chesters, Robbie had sometimes nearly forgotten he wasn't their son. But then someone would say or do something, an invitation would come for "the family", and Robbie would be left home. Such small matters reminded him of the distance between them. He was not a guest or employee, and he *was* a part of the family, but never quite a full-fledged member.

"Very well," he answered as he realized his silence had gone on too long. He spoke absently, not truly heeding his own response. "When the time is right for the transition, I will step aside. You're right, Uncle Phillip. It is time I made my own way in the world."

Charles's head pounded and his eyes seemed to be glued shut. A thick, foul-tasting substance coated his mouth. His legs were stiff and throbbing with pain. If he opened his eyes, he knew everything would only hurt worse. Any ray of sunlight sneaking between the heavy drapes at the windows would spear into his head like a knife and finish him off. Maybe he should continue to lie here until the blessed dark of night resumed.

But life went on. A man couldn't hide from reality under the bedcovers like a child fearing monsters in dark corners. And he couldn't drink away reality either.

Charles peeled open his eyes and sat. He waited until the thumping in his head subsided, then swung his legs over the edge of the bed. Sucking in a breath, he put his feet on the floor and stood, holding on to the edge of the bed for balance. And then he let go and continued to stand.

Standing. On his own two feet. Everything would be all right. He would become himself again.

It took only the length of time for that thought to enter his head before his legs buckled and he fell. Luckily, the wheeled chair was close beside the bed. He caught an arm of the heavy thing on the way down and heaved himself back into its confines.

All right. So his weakened legs wouldn't hold him yet. But at least he was no longer having those strange symptoms he'd suffered from over the last months—the ones that had led to the carriage accident. His legs had turned to jelly, and he'd stumbled a few times. And then the symptoms had grown worse. Numb extremities, loss of control over his muscles. One day he'd woken on the floor after one of those fits of weakness drooling, for God's sake! Demeaning, debilitating, and no doctor could find a thing wrong with him.

His friend, a doctor, had suggested a good sanitarium, and Charles soon realized he'd meant an insane asylum.

"You have a vivid imagination," his friend had explained gently. That conversation had taken place even before the worst of the illness had robbed him of everything. Fear of losing control like that again swept through him. Whatever the strange illness had been, it had stricken him out of the blue. What if it were to happen again?

But no. He couldn't think that way. He'd never before lived his life in fear, and he wasn't about to start now.

And all of that drinking? No. Not prompted by fear. He refused to consider such an idea.

Charles pushed at the wheels of the chair and moved himself several feet across the floor. He was just trying to figure out how he'd get to his clothing and dress himself when there was a knock at the door.

"Come in." He looked up and was unreasonably disappointed when the footman, Stewart, and not Cousin Robbie entered the room. "Ah, so they've assigned you to be my valet, or is it caretaker? Sorry about that and about the trouble I caused last night."

Apologies to a servant? The old Charles would never have given a thought to any mess he made for someone else to clean up.

"That's fine, sir. I'm glad to help." Stewart moved about quickly, helping Charles wash and dress, then pushed the unwieldy chair out of the room, careful not to scrape the doorframe on the way through.

Cleaned and clothed, Charles felt leagues better than he had the previous night. Sunlight shone through windowpanes, illuminating the breakfast room, and he fell upon the kippers and eggs, toast and tea with a hearty appetite, wishing there were sausages as well.

The room was quiet but for the clinking of fork against plate. None of the Chesters appeared, and Charles wondered how much in disgrace he was with the family. Stewart stood nearby to wait on him as needed.

"Do you think you might push me outdoors for a bit of fresh air?" Questions instead of commands were apparently the new order. *No longer the master of the house*—yet he could contemplate that fact without the bitterness it usually engendered. Perhaps his lack of rancor could be the result of a good breakfast, the first he'd had in weeks. Bankruptcy tended to make meals less consistent.

"I'm afraid I can't, sir. I have other duties to attend to."

"Oh, of course," Charles said airily as if he had no true interest in going outside. "Then perhaps I should return to my, ah, room." The converted library seemed as good a place as any for imprisonment. Better than most. All those books he'd never had time to read during his past active life.

"All right then." After a long pause, Stewart added, "Sir."

Charles suppressed a sigh and wondered if he could find a book on the topic of how to conduct oneself as an infirm and possibly brain-addled houseguest. Perhaps he might write such a monograph.

Rule one: *A dependent must not notice any rudeness or neglect.* No, the first rule must be *do not arrive drunk as a sailor,* quickly followed by rule number two, *if one must be sick, locate an appropriate container.*

The door to the breakfast room opened, and there stood Robert Grayson, who didn't wear a smile.

Rule three: *Do not lust after members of the household.*

Chapter Four

Robbie still felt the shock of his uncle's words roiling through him. He wouldn't belong here. He had been dismissed, or would be soon. Irrational fear clutched him and held him so hard he had to walk outside. He stumbled through the rose garden, looking for the refuge of the small maze.

The boxwoods had not grown tall enough yet to hide the paths. He'd always supposed he'd still be here when they grew taller.

He'd forgotten his cane, and when he sat on the stone bench heavily, he immediately wondered how he would haul himself back up again.

Something to worry about in two minutes. Now he must face his more distant future.

Not a part of the family, not working for the estate. He swallowed hard and tried to recall the time he'd wanted to leave.

Two years ago, he'd departed of his own will. That time, his uncle had flatly declared he could not easily spare Robbie, yet Robbie had gone. He'd tried to explain his ambition. Lenore and Gemma had cried, Phillip had grown grim, and, despite his guilt, Robbie had chosen to go to London. A fortnight later, he had been fetched back home, nearly dead from influenza.

Until he'd grown ill, London had meant freedom. *Recall the pleasure of that short experience,* he scolded himself. He could easily summon the delight of those few days working with the great designer M. Reynaud. He'd learned so much about space and dimensions and the use of color, fabrics and lighting in designing a space that his head felt full to bursting with knowledge. In fact, at first Robbie had imagined his severe headaches to be the result of too much knowledge crammed into his brain. By the time he was diagnosed with influenza, Robbie was out of his mind with fever and transported back to the hall to recover.

Today everything had changed.

Uncle Phillip no longer tried to stop him from pursuing his dream. Now his uncle pushed the bird from the nest. The cuckoo. Robbie smiled. Perhaps it was his uncle's easy willingness to let him go that woke Robbie's hesitation.

"Perverse creature," he scolded himself. He picked a small twig of the boxwood and fit the tip of his finger into the rounded leaf.

Freedom beckoned again. Except he could not move into a new life immediately. He had two jobs: help Samuel learn his duties, and take care of the troublesome Worthington cousin. Which one would form the greatest obstacle to a peaceful life? Samuel taking instruction from him seemed a ridiculous notion. But worse, much worse—Charles Worthington. When Robbie pictured Worthington, his breath seemed to clog his throat.

The mere thought of tending the man's physical requirements aroused him. Robbie thumped his leg, hoping the pain would teach his body to stop useless longing. Dear God, if the sight of Worthington sick and—what was the phrase Stewart had used?—a sick and sloppy souse hadn't been enough to drive away the pangs of desire, Robbie was a lost man.

And that made no matter. He would do his duty.

He managed to lever himself up and off the bench and started back to the house. A momentary flash of dislike for Worthington coursed through him as he slowly, carefully walked. That blundering, too-attractive man now presented a barrier to his peace and to his goals.

Before he reached the front door, shame for his selfishness followed. Poor Worthington didn't know how he affected Robbie, and he certainly hadn't heard that Robbie was obligated to help with his recovery.

Robbie stopped to fetch his cane from the umbrella stand where the maids stuffed it. Had he calmed sufficiently to approach Worthington with a steady manner? Two more breaths, and he went to the breakfast room.

It was almost a disappointment to see nothing but the empty table with its chairs drawn tight.

He met the younger footman, Jacob, in the hall. "Do you know where Mr. Worthington is?"

"The sot?"

He almost nodded but knew that he must check the insolence. "That is inappropriate. Mr. Worthington is our guest, a member of the family, and should be treated with respect." He kept his voice quiet and, he hoped, stern.

"Sorry, sir." Jacob grinned at him.

Good enough, he supposed. He allowed himself the nod and then walked on, slightly shaken by the interaction. By the time he realized he hadn't gotten an answer, Jacob had disappeared.

Robbie found Worthington in the library. He sat in his chair with a stack of books next to him.

The invalid's face lit when he saw Robbie. "Mr. Grayson! Just the man I wanted to see."

"Oh?"

"Yes, I owe apologies to every creature in this place, and I think most of all I owe you one or two or a thousand."

Any scrap of resentment about having to act as this man's nursemaid vanished. He couldn't resist that smile. The other emotion, desire, remained damnably steady.

"Not at all." Robbie walked over and sat in the wooden desk chair near him. Not too near. "My uncle has asked me to help you in any way I can. I know it is dreadfully prying, but perhaps you can share the details of your injury?" Robbie raised his eyebrows, inviting full disclosure.

Uncle Phillip hadn't shared many details, but Robbie knew that this man had lost everything. Worthington's branch of the family had once been even wealthier than Mr. Phillip Chester's own. Surely a pair of broken legs would not be enough to send anyone over the edge into bankruptcy. Could Worthington have succumbed to drink or melancholia? Was he a gambler? Robbie hoped he'd get an answer, but judging from the man's suddenly grave and unreadable expression, he didn't think he'd find out the details.

"It wasn't just broken tibias," Worthington said, then fell silent.

Robbie waited. The clock ticked.

"Damnation, I've also been ill," Worthington said angrily, as if he thought Robbie might not believe him.

"I am sorry," Robbie soothed.

Worthington laughed, then shook his head. "I beg your pardon. I don't mean to attack you."

"I'm not offended." He considered what he might say that would not sound patronizing or pitying. "I know that illness and pain can affect one's outlook. That's what I heard in your words, not an attack on me."

"Yes. You're observant, Mr. Grayson. I hope you haven't learned too much of that lesson from your own experiences." Worthington's smile showed even, white teeth. Good lord, he must have been irresistible before his illness, and he was used to his effect on people. Even pale and bony, he had the easy charismatic air of a man who knew people would like him or at least admire his looks.

"A little," Robbie said. "I mean, I contracted something called poliomyelitis as a child, but I've long since recovered, or as better as I shall ever get." He wiggled the cane at his side to indicate the cursed lasting effects. He didn't want to speak of his own illness. It had nothing to do with Worthington or his recovery. "You are still ill?"

Worthington leaned back in his chair with a thump. "If you're asking *me,* the answer is yes."

"And who else might I ask?"

"Doctors. Although I suppose they're generous enough to grant me some form of illness, they'd tell you it was here." He tapped his head.

Robbie gawped at him. Madness? Surely no, although he didn't know why he would entirely reject the diagnosis.

Never mind, the origin didn't matter. If Worthington felt symptoms, they must be addressed. And perhaps he wasn't indicating a case of insanity. "Are you saying you're giddy?" he asked.

Worthington's angry, suspicious glare melted. He laughed. "Yes, actually that is on the list. Headaches and dizziness are among my symptoms. Shall I give you the laundry list?"

Robbie spread his hands. "Please do."

The list was impressive, but Robbie noticed one encouraging fact. "You often speak in the past tense. Many of these symptoms are gone now?"

Worthington nodded. "Yes, but occasionally I've celebrated the end of some horrifically embarrassing symptom and then it's shown up again, rejoining the party." He folded his arms over his chest. "I am not imagining these things, Mr. Grayson."

"Of course you're not imagining them." Robbie felt impatient. "Did you want to argue about the causes of your symptoms? I can go fetch our local physician if you wish for that sort of conversation. I'm no doctor. In fact, judging from your ability to reset my shoulder, I'd say you were a thousand times more likely to be mistaken for one than I am."

Worthington laughed. "Do you know, I thought you were a mousy sort of a person when we met?"

"That was only yesterday. And yes, I recall you added me into a Burns poem."

"I was wrong. You're not cowardly at all."

"I am, but I don't give a fig about it." Robbie waved a dismissive hand. "I'm not here to discuss my lack of courage."

"Why are you here?"

"To help you."

Worthington canted sideways in his chair. That slow, seductive smile spread. "And why on earth are you interested in me? I get the impression that you're a busy man."

Now was the time to put distance between them. He would. He must. "Because my uncle asked me to help you."

The smile only faltered a little. "But I don't think you'll mind spending time with me. I think we'll have fun."

Really. The man did have a strong opinion of himself. Robbie longed to point out that, so far, their time together consisted of Robbie cleaning up his sick, hardly what anyone would call fun.

Worthington went on, "Do you meet a lot of people near your age here at Chester Hall? Do you go on picnics with them?"

"I'm not a social creature, Mr. Worthington."

"No, I suppose you haven't had that opportunity."

"I am content." Really, this wasn't how the conversation was supposed to go.

"I'm not surprised. I think your natural instinct is to help others."

"Just as yours is to change the subject. Tell me, do your symptoms grow better or worse depending on your level of activity?"

"When I'm tired, they're worse. But come, we've already talked about the dreary illness. Let's discuss something more interesting. What are your dreams, Mr. Grayson?"

What an odd question. Had anyone ever asked him before? Not that he could remember—certainly never with any intention to actually listen to the answer. And such a questioner—tousle-haired as if he'd just come from bed, with those intelligent brown eyes concentrating on him, on Robbie.

Oh Lord. He had never understood that focused attention could so easily seduce a person. No. He wouldn't allow yearning to pierce him.

"My dreams are my own," he said softly. "And I'm afraid they aren't very interesting."

Worthington's eyes sparkled. "You should allow me to be the judge."

Robbie couldn't move, caught by the man.

And then Gemma's familiar little voice came from not far away. She must have walked into the library without making a sound. That was impossible with those hard little shoes on the wood floors, so Robbie had been too captivated to hear her.

"Please, please don't tell Mama, Robbie. But I wanted to meet my cousin."

"Is this my Cousin Gemma?" Worthington leaned forward, his hand outstretched. "I am delighted to meet you. I was dreadfully ill yesterday and in no shape to be introduced to a lady."

"You were drunk," she said solemnly. "Disgracefully, utterly drunk." Robbie wondered if she quoted Mary or her new governess, Miss Peters.

He ought to point out that she shouldn't say such things, but Worthington said, "Yes, I was. Drinking to excess is a stupid thing to do. I advise against it."

He had her hand and raised it to his lips for an elegant, exaggerated salute, the perfect move to entertain a lady of any age.

Gemma giggled.

Of course, Charles Worthington had moved in stylish circles in his former life. No doubt once upon a time he could enchant ballrooms and speak easily with anyone.

Robbie supposed he should go find the nursemaid, Mary or Miss Peters. Aunt Lenore would not be pleased by innocent Gemma talking to Worthington.

The house was big, but could they really expect to keep Gemma separated from Worthington? Not if she was determined to seek him out, so Robbie saw no point in dragging her away. He would solve the problem by not leaving them alone.

Worthington focused intently on his small cousin now, asking her solemn questions about her lessons, her interests, the fascinating puppies in the kennel.

Seeing Worthington turn his charm on the child, Robbie realized the man's similar keen interest in him meant little. It was merely Worthington's manner. Good thing Robbie hadn't allowed himself to be seduced into attraction. Even entirely private longing thoughts must be avoided.

Once the initial realization and inexplicable disappointment that Worthington was naturally flirtatious had passed, Robbie listened with amusement as Gemma described her favorite puppy and Worthington discussed the best ways to sneak the animal into a disapproving household. How could a man this charismatic not save himself from his creditors?

"You shouldn't encourage her." He joined the conversation. "The last time Gemma brought in one of her favorites, it piddled on several of the best carpets and chewed Uncle Phillip's favorite pipe."

"You forgot that she was sick all over the floor in here." Gemma sounded proud.

"This library seems to attract that sort of behavior," murmured Worthington with a look at Robbie. "The worst visitors find their way here."

"I shall go and find Daisy again and introduce her to you, Cousin Charles. She's ever so adorable." The child ran to the door and was gone.

Robbie began to pull himself up. "I suspect I should go stop her."

"No, don't. Let the girl get into some mischief."

Robbie laughed. "She will manage on her own or with Bertie's help." He didn't go after her, though.

Worthington watched him again, but Robbie knew better than to fall into that hypnotic gaze. "I think perhaps I should give you a tour. I doubt I can push your chair, but I will find Stewart or Jacob or fetch Forrester."

"Your shoulder still hurts?"

Robbie nodded.

"Did I apologize for that?"

"Indeed you did, more than once. Let's forget all about yesterday, shall we? Start with a fresh slate."

"No. That's a terrible idea. Forgetting has been my goal, and I think I shouldn't even try." The light died from his face, and Worthington slowly shook his head. "I have drunk too much lately. You say you want to help me, Robbie Grayson? *Don't* let me forget yesterday."

The sunlight felt like warm honey trickling over his face. Charles tipped his head back and simply reveled in the sweet nectar of fresh air and sunshine as Forrester propelled his chair along bumpy garden paths.

Charles opened his eyes and glanced at the figure of Robbie Grayson before him. There was no room for the big, clumsy chair and a man to move abreast, but that was fine with Charles. He enjoyed the rear view of his non-cousin. The man's leg might be lame from early lack of development, but his shoulders were wide enough to fill out his coat nicely, and his back was erect. His halting gait did not detract from the sight of narrow hips and a slim backside beneath his trousers. He couldn't help thinking of the man as Robbie rather than Mr. Grayson. Such an interesting set of contrasts. For instance, he dressed in somber, almost Puritanical hues, yet there was something rather playful about the man. The clothes designed for a much older man hid that lighter side of Robbie. Charles was no clotheshorse, but he did appreciate flare and wished he could see Robbie dressed in more fashionable attire.

"As you can see, the gardens have been encouraged to grow in a more natural manner rather than the rigid lines of classic formal gardens." Robbie glanced over his shoulder. "I admit to taking a bit of a hand in the redesign of the gardens. My aunt always had little interest in gardening, and my uncle none at all. Since the space didn't matter to them, they allowed me free rein here."

Charles looked around at the abundant foliage of topiary and ornamental trees, broken by open spaces in a harmonious blend. The views were pleasing to the eye. "A beautiful job. So you've an eye toward landscape design?"

Robbie didn't answer immediately but continued to stride forward, leaving Charles to wonder if he'd heard. Then he glanced back again. "Designing interiors, actually. While studying at university, I realized how much I enjoyed the creation of a space. I found I had a gift for making a plain room inviting and assisted some fellows I knew in making their flats more pleasant."

Some fellows. Was that code for special friends? Or did he know the teaching staff at the university? Charles wondered.

"And yet you returned to help your uncle with estate business." Charles worked at piecing together Robbie's life story. "I presume you felt it your duty after all he'd done for you." A debt that he too now owed Cousin Phillip.

"Not precisely." Robbie turned away again so his voice was a bit muffled and Charles couldn't see his expressive face as he talked. "After I graduated university, I moved to London, where I was apprenticed to the designer M. Reynaud. But I was there only a very brief time before I fell ill with influenza and had to return home."

Charles frowned and wished good old Forrester would push the chair faster. He wanted to stay closer to Robbie. Actually, he wanted Robbie to turn around so he could see his face.

"Then why are you still here? Monsieur Reynaud didn't save a place for you?"

Robbie's shoulders moved up and down in a small but eloquent shrug. "Too much time had passed. Such a prime opportunity to learn at the feet of a master was filled by the next eager student. Besides, Uncle Phillip required my help. It was the least I could do."

His statement actually raised more questions for Charles. Why had Robbie been so indispensable? What really kept him from making another try at the world outside this country estate? Charles felt certain there was more to the story than what he'd learned, and his eagerness to unravel the mysteries of Robbie increased.

"Wait up! Wait for me." A high little voice called from some distance.

Charles turned in the chair, craning to see around Forrester's generous figure. The big coachman stepped aside.

"Miss Gemma, what did I say about leaving the pups with their mother?" Forrester said. "They're too young to be carried around."

The little girl came huffing up, red-faced from exertion and clutching something to her chest. "I just have to show Daisy to Mr. Worthington. I promised. But you didn't wait for me." She glared at Robbie and Charles. "After I went to all the trouble of sneaking her into the library."

"Sorry, darling." Charles knew how to please women both young and old. They appreciated apologies for any slight, real or imagined. He opened his hands as the child came close, and she thrust a squirming bundle of doggery at him.

He wasn't a great pet enthusiast, but he had to admit the tan-and-white puppy snuffling in his lap was rather charming—until it piddled a few drops on his trousers. He offered the animal back to Gemma. "Very sweet."

Robbie came over and stooped to rest a hand on Gemma's shoulder while petting the puppy. "You should probably take Daisy back to her mum. I think she's hungry."

Gemma pressed her own small nose against the dog's wet, black one. "You didn't wait for me," she repeated. "Neither did Bertie. He's gone off without me again. He never wants to play with me anymore." She looked up at Robbie, and tears shone in her eyes. "He hates me now."

Robbie lowered himself to an awkward crouch to talk to her. "Bertie's growing up. It's natural for him to wish to spend time with boys his own age like Liam. But you mustn't think he doesn't love you. He's your big brother, and he will always care for you."

"But he still won't play with me or take me to the woods," she grumbled. "I have to stay at home with boring old Mary, who won't let me have any fun."

Almost as she said it, a white-aproned figure emerged from a side door of the great stone house and hurried toward the garden, calling Gemma's name.

"I'm afraid you've conjured your nanny," Charles teased, trying to amuse the sad little girl. "Are you certain you're not a witch?"

The rather rotund Mary stopped walking and called from a distance, "Gemma. Miss Gemma. You must come inside directly. Come along now, miss. But first put that pup back where it belongs!"

"Robbie..." Gemma pleaded.

If she'd directed those liquid blue eyes at Charles, he would've melted and allowed her to linger. But apparently Robbie was made of sterner stuff. He pretended to steal her nose, his thumb tip emerging between two fingers, and Gemma smiled.

"Sorry, my sweet. Mary calls, and you must go. But I promise...I *swear* to spend time with you later this afternoon. Perhaps we might play a game."

"All right." The little martyr turned and trudged forlornly toward her prison guard in the white cap and apron.

"Poor wee mite," Forrester muttered. "Her brother's grown past her, and they were so close when they were small."

"Nothing so fleeting as childhood." Robbie watched his little cousin walk away. He stood so close that Charles could feel the warmth of his body, hear the whisper of fabric when he moved, smell a faint odor of starch from his shirt and something else, something earthier and manlier. Robbie's nearness disconcerted Charles.

"I should like to see more of the grounds, but perhaps Mr. Forrester is tired of pushing me," Charles said. "Besides, I feel it's time to meet my responsibilities and apologize to my cousin and his wife for my deplorable behavior yesterday." He glanced up at the big man propelling the ponderous chair. "Will you wheel me inside, please, Forrester."

"Yes, sir."

"You shall find Uncle Phillip in his study," Robbie said. "Aunt Lenore will likely be in her sitting room, tatting lace or perhaps planning meals with Cook."

"Lovely. How shall I manage the stairs?"

"I expect you may have to wait until they come down to tea."

"Right. Best to get the apologies over with *en masse.*" Charles wrinkled his nose. "I presume Cousin Lenore won't be easily thawed."

"Oh, she's not bad," Robbie said. "She tends to believe the best in people. Tell her you don't drink as a habit and prostrate yourself in greatest remorse, figuratively speaking, and she will be mollified."

Charles grinned at Robbie's teasing tone. This man he'd immediately assumed to be stodgy turned out to be an intriguing mix of starchy and relaxed. His subversive sense of humor coupled with a warm generosity of spirit were delightful.

And he smelled good.

Robbie continued. "You might take advantage of this afternoon to work on building your strength. There are exercises I was given long ago to help regain mobility in my legs. They might be of use to you."

"Yes. I would appreciate that." And more time spent in Robbie's company, this time without a servant in attendance. "But I thought you helped Phillip with accounts or some such."

"We have a new bailiff who has taken over some of my duties, and when Samuel returns, he will assume his rightful place at his father's side."

Charles couldn't see Robbie's face, as the man still walked a few steps before him, but he detected a hint of displeasure. "Well, that works out rather well, doesn't it? Maybe you will be able to resume your original plans, or something like."

He fell silent a moment. "Yes, perhaps. Samuel shall learn how to care for the estate. Between him and Mr. Todd, the bailiff, there will be no further need of my services."

"Ah, I see." Charles easily understood that rather disgruntled tone. Robbie had grown used to being needed. He would soon be free to pursue his own desires at last and was both hurt at his easy replacement and afraid of the future.

His woes were an exact counterpart to Charles's. As Charles dreaded his narrowing options and acclimating himself to this smaller world, Robbie feared shedding his cocoon and stretching his wings. Ironic. What Charles could teach him about the possibilities of a dizzying pace of the city and the fun to be had.

An idea struck. A way to repay this man for his kindness. While Robbie helped him regain his strength and the ability to walk, Charles would offer something in return. Not overtly, but in subtle ways, he could teach Robbie how to fit into London society. That was the ticket. A project to keep him entertained during his recovery, and a mission to help his inexperienced new friend launch a voyage into the grander world. Despite his penniless state, he still had some sway with influential folk in London—and he vowed to use his connections to help Robbie.

Chapter Five

"Fourteen. That's it. You're doing well. Fifteen. Only five more... Sixteen..."

Robbie prattled encouragement and tried to pretend he wasn't holding Worthington's legs while the man's feet rested against his chest. But he could feel the warm spot each stocking-clad foot pressed into his skin even through his shirt and vest, and the weight and heft of Worthington's calves in his hands were distracting to say the least. The flex of muscles as Charles repeated each exercise sent little thrills through Robbie.

Sick to think so about a damaged man struggling to recover, but try as he might, Robbie couldn't halt the desires percolating inside him, a thick brew that would taste so bitter and yet so sweet if he only dared sip it.

"All right. Enough." He spoke to himself more than to Charles as he set the man's legs back on the large Turkish carpet which covered the library floor. "No need to push too hard. You've only been at it for a week."

"A week of torture," Charles gasped as he flopped backward with his arms spread wide. His white undershirt and pale body made a stark and intriguing contrast to the burgundy carpet with its intricate geometric designs. It was all Robbie could do not to stare.

"I believe you're enjoying this too much," Charles added.

"No. No, I'm not," Robbie said hastily, and flushed as he realized Charles was joking. "These stretching exercises may not seem like much exertion but will bring energy back into your legs, allowing them to heal more quickly."

"Oh, trust me, the exercises feel like plenty of exertion." Charles wiped a hand across his damp forehead. "Worse than a fencing lesson."

"You fence? I've always admired that sport, though I haven't had an opportunity to observe often. It's beautiful to watch the movements. Like a hectic dance." *A dance with graceful, well-muscled men.* He was glad Worthington couldn't see into his perverted mind.

"I could teach you both when I'm on my feet again, which I no longer have any doubt I will be, thanks to your expert care."

Robbie felt a stab of impatience. Surely the man didn't think someone with Robbie's physical flaws could either dance or fence? Charles would eventually recover his balance and stamina. Robbie never would. But the flash of hurt came and went quickly. It always did.

"These are only preliminary strengthening exercises. You have a long road to recovery before you."

"Yes. I realize that." Charles waved it away with a casual flick of the wrist.

The invalid wallowing in misery and liquor whom Robbie had first met had disappeared. Robbie felt he was seeing the true Charles Worthington, the man as he was before his accident and loss of almost everything he possessed. Such a man took life as it came, grabbed it and wrestled with it if need be, but always came out on top. Robbie could study a page from his book and adopt a bolder character when he ventured out into the world.

"Water, please," Charles said.

Robbie scrambled up to get the pitcher and glass from the low bookshelf that had been dragged from a corner to act as a night table. Just as well to put a little distance between them.

Sitting on his heels in front of Charles's supine body felt too oddly provocative. Too close and too intimate. He offered Charles the glass and then sat on a nearby settee.

"So," Charles said after he'd drained the glass. "Do you think Cousin Lenore has truly forgiven me? I was as profuse and lavish with the apologies as I could possibly be."

"Which she greatly appreciated, though she's still not keen on you spending much time around Gemma or Bert." Robbie smiled. "But she has begun to make plans for us concerning the harvest ball, so you can't be too much in her bad graces."

Charles quirked an eyebrow, and Robbie's heart skipped a beat. Such a small thing, and yet Charles's ability to easily arch one eyebrow simply made him giddy.

"What in the world are you talking about?"

"The harvest ball which is hosted in turns by various gentry in the district. It's the gala event of the season here. It is the Chesters' year for it. "

"I see." Charles stretched, braced his hands behind him and carefully pushed up to a sitting position. "And what is Lenore's great plan that concerns you and me?"

"Because we can't dance, we are to partner a pair of aging spinsters, the Brown sisters. We are to make them feel admired and squired, even though we are unable to dance with them. You and I will be their playthings for the evening."

"Ah." Charles rotated his head, cracking his neck with an audible pop, then stretched his arms in one direction and his torso in another. Robbie watched, mesmerized by the sinuous movement.

"I will admit I have been called on to 'make the numbers' at a social event more than once in my life, but it's been years," Charles said. "I gave up on such awkward conventions and pursued my own desires over the past few years."

"Oh?" Robbie wanted to hear more about Charles's dissolute and probably fascinating life, but the man didn't elaborate, and it didn't seem good form to pry.

"I may be stuck in a chair, but there's no reason *you* can't enjoy yourself at this harvest ball and flirt with women other than the spinsters we're meant to entertain."

"Between my lame leg and orphan status, I'm hardly considered a catch amongst the local young ladies."

"Then they are fools not to look past surface flaws, for you possess all the qualities any sane woman would be glad to have in a husband."

Robbie laughed as he rose, then fussed about, tidying the books Charles had left in a careless pile by the bed, avoiding any glimpse of Charles's vibrant face.

That face would do him in, making him desire things that he could never have and should not want. It roused all sorts of dark feelings he'd mostly managed to push deep down for years. Helping Charles with these exercises every day and having such long, friendly conversations made the desires grow stronger. Yet he couldn't avoid Charles, because Phillip wanted him to aid the man. What to do?

"I believe Gemma would greatly love a game of Snap. Shall I go find her and the cards?" Yes, anything to put a buffer between them.

"If you like. Or we might sit and play a game of chess, just you and I. After you help me into my chair, that is."

"Right. Sorry." Robbie hastened to drag Charles upright and into the wheelchair. Charles wasn't a dead weight but Robbie had to wrestle with the other man's greater height and weight, and the proximity with that muscular body left Robbie with his clothes disheveled and his spirit even more so.

"I, um. I'll get out the chess pieces." He was so flustered he forgot for a moment where he was. He started to head toward the door, remembered that both the inlaid chess table and the marble pieces were in the room, and spun around to retrieve the box from within the window seat. He focused on setting up the board and regaining his wits. When he glanced up, Charles had wheeled himself over to the table. He was getting stronger.

Worthington cocked his head and looked up at Robbie. "What's the matter, Cousin? You seem a bit winded, as if you were the one who'd been exercising."

"Not your cousin," Robbie said shortly. "And there's nothing wrong with me. Simply looking forward to a rousing game of chess."

"Ah yes, the anticipation of such an exciting match has got me on pins and needles too." Charles matched his dry tone. "Could you help me steer a little closer to the table? I think I've gone as far as I'm able."

"Of course." Robbie moved behind Charles and pushed him up to the parquet game table set in front of a large window. Usually the drapes were drawn to protect the library from sunlight. Robbie had tied them back with tasseled ropes, allowing a golden glow to fall on the glossy wood table some long-dead, chess-loving Chester had crafted.

Standing behind the wheelchair, he could look down at the crown of Charles's head and the way his hair swirled in a perfect spiral from one point. Such thick auburn hair. It crackled with hints of red fire and seemed as if it would be hot to the touch. Oh God, how badly he wanted to do just that, stroke lightly and then plunge his fingers through the fine strands. And then to touch that strong neck, the muscle in the side, right...there! Robbie's cock began to quicken.

He stepped back, discreetly adjusted the bulge in his trousers and took his seat across from Charles.

The only solution to this torture was to focus on the game, and Robbie did so with a vengeance. He matched Charles's every move with aggressive counterattacks and in short order had the other man's queen pinned.

Charles studied the bloody battlefield and grunted in dismay. He rested his fingertip on the king and pushed over the piece. "I can see I need to strengthen my game play as well as my legs. I hope you'll continue to help me with both. Don't see how I could do it without you."

His tone telegraphed another of those silent messages to Robbie, the sort of message that tingled up and down his spine. Coupled with the long, steady *look* Charles gave him, there was little doubt the man was...flirting was the only word that came to mind.

"Yes. Well. That is..." Good Lord, his babbling was back. "Uncle Phillip ordered me to help you during your recovery, and so I suppose I shall keep doing so."

"Ordered?" Charles's voice was flat.

Robbie wished he hadn't been quite so blunt, but he was desperate to put a fence between them. Apparently he'd erected a wall.

"You're helping me only because your beloved uncle asked you to do it?" Worthington reiterated, but this time there was a challenge in his tone.

"I don't mind. I mean, I like helping you out, and, um, spending time with you. It's quite...pleasant." Embarrassment heated his face. He hadn't meant to make Charles feel like a chore or unwanted. God, no. He'd only meant to cover up how very *much* he wanted Charles.

"That's all right. I understand," Charles said coolly. He pushed on the huge chair wheels with all his strength, his biceps bulging under his shirtsleeves, and the chair inched away from the table.

"Here. I can help you." Robbie leaped from his seat, eager to push Charles wherever he wanted to go, wishing he could take back the suggestion that Charles was a burden and return to the camaraderie they'd enjoyed over the past week together.

"No. That's quite all right. I've become quite capable of manipulating my own wheelchair."

"Please, don't... I'm sorry." Robbie felt breathless, shaken and infinitely regretful.

"For what?" Charles swiveled in his seat and gazed up at Robbie with fiery eyes. "For being a good host to your pathetic invalid relative? Or for looking at said relative with desire?"

Robbie wondered if he'd misheard the words. "I don't understand," he tried, but fell silent because he wasn't sure he wanted to hear that thought voiced aloud again.

Charles snorted. "You're hiding. I'm not sure if you're lying to me or to both of us."

"No." Robbie had to defend himself from this outrageous charge, especially because it was too true. "You are mistaken."

"Don't think I can't see the hunger in your eyes. I'm crippled, not blind. Phillip may have told you to aid me, but you want to do it anyway. You can't admit the real reason why. It's not altruism or sympathy for a fellow cripple. You *want* to be near me. And by the by, you're a terrible liar. I suppose that's part of your appeal. Honesty is such an alluring trait."

Robbie was at last rendered speechless. He couldn't believe Charles had actually given voice to the veiled inklings of lust that had shot between them practically since they'd met. It was like kerosene poured on a fire that raged into a towering bonfire. How had this change occurred so quickly? Two minutes ago, they'd been talking about chess!

"I don't... I'm not..." Robbie floundered. "I don't know what you're talking about."

"You know damn well what I'm talking about. Stop denying it." Charles gripped the arms of his chair so hard his knuckles were white. And his face was turning a dark red to match his hair.

"No." Robbie tried again. "I couldn't begin to think that way. It's—"

The library door flew open and nearly crashed against the wall.

Both men looked toward the noise.

A tall young man with the fair hair and erect carriage of his father and the deep blue eyes of his mother walked into the room. "Hello there, Cousin. I'm home. And you must be my—is it second cousin?—Charles. Pleased to meet you. I'm Samuel."

Chapter Six

Charles wanted to laugh. He enjoyed farce, although perhaps not when he was pitchforked into the middle of it. And not when Robbie's face had drawn into a tight, unhappy blankness. Had Charles done that with his confrontation or was it young Samuel's presence that made the man vanish into himself?

He wheeled away from Robbie and toward the newcomer. "How are you, Samuel?"

The young man graced him with a nod. "I'm tired after my journey from France. Lord, what a time I've had." His careless manner seemed unstudied. Samuel was either a fine actor, or he hadn't overheard their conversation.

Charles said, "Pardon me for not rising to greet you. We have met, although you were very young at the time—perhaps Gemma's age." He grinned up at his cousin.

Samuel didn't smile back. He took Charles's proffered hand and squeezed it far too tightly for a polite exchange of greetings. Had the young master heard of his disgraceful drunken arrival or was he simply aggressive for no real reason?

For a brief moment, less than a second, Charles considered what he should do. Allow the blighter to injure his hand and back down from the challenge— or fight the unspoken expression of dominance?

He squeezed back, hard.

Samuel released his grip almost at once. One handshake demonstrated that Samuel would be a nuisance but probably a controllable one.

At the moment, Charles worried more about Robbie. He cursed himself for losing his temper just before Samuel appeared. He shouldn't have been hurt by the fact that Robbie claimed to help him only from a sense of obligation. The fact that it did prickle him worried Charles a little.

Ah well, Robbie wasn't going anywhere. Charles had time enough to retreat and try again with more élan. Or perhaps he should retreat entirely and concentrate solely on recovering his strength and finding how he could make his way in the world. He damned well wasn't going to impinge upon his relations a moment longer than he had to.

"Have you enjoyed your exhausting life at university, Samuel?"

"Lord, yes, and my tour of Europe even more so." He walked around the library, now bedroom, stopping beside the bed and makeshift night table to grunt his distaste at the changes. "But now I'm back here. Back to stay, I should think."

Samuel's words, the way he swaggered about the library, all seemed like a threat directed at the two others in the room. Charles felt his mouth twitch into an involuntary grin. During his long, dreary days shut up in his slowly emptying house, he'd raided McNair's penny dreadful collection for entertainment. Samuel reminded him of a sheriff in one of the American Western stories, threatening the evil-doers who'd come to town looking for trouble. Or perhaps Samuel was one of the gunslingers bent on breaking the lawmen?

"And are you glad to be home?" he asked.

"Yes. I am." Distaste still evident on his fine features, Samuel watched Robbie, who was placing the chess pieces back in their box. Surely the topic of Samuel taking his place in the family business no longer disturbed Robbie. Why was his head ducked, and why on earth did he look as if he loathed each little carved figure he touched?

Did Phillip know his son and ward disliked each other or felt some other antagonistic tension? If Charles could see it in five seconds, surely everyone in the family knew.

He knew the cousins didn't suffer from the sort of tension Charles and Robbie inflicted upon each other—he understood that down to his bones. Thank God for that.

Phillip must have an imp in his head to set these two up against each other in competition. Charles wondered if Samuel knew his father's plans. Easy enough to find out.

"Cousin Samuel, it will be a shame that just as you come home, Mr. Grayson will move on to his new life."

Samuel's start was almost comical.

He and Robbie turned to stare at Charles, who gave a dismissive shrug.

"Oh, of course he won't leave right away. Didn't you say you're supposed to tutor your cousin in estate matters, Mr. Grayson?"

"These plans are still forming." The look of disgust Robbie directed at him was pointed. This man had a dislike for plain speaking.

Charles reflected that though an invalid should take entertainment where he could, he should stop needling Robbie, or he might be abandoned.

"My mistake, then," Charles said.

Samuel took another circuit of the room. He glared at a marble bust of Shakespeare, lifted the lid of the Majolica cigar humidor, then put it down with a clink that threatened to crack the pottery.

He took a very long minute to examine the armoire and trunk hauled down from the attic to hold Charles's small collection of belongings.

"Hardly suitable furnishings for a library." Samuel's nose wrinkled with distaste.

"This arrangement is temporary," Robbie said.

"Very well." Samuel waved a hand as if dismissing the matter. "Lord, I'm hungry. I'll see you at tea, I expect," he said in that irritating manner of a young man who knows he's vastly superior to the people he addresses. Charles suddenly understood there were advantages to succumbing to illness, injury and helplessness. The humility they created stopped one from behaving like that young fool.

He watched the replica of himself from a year earlier saunter from the library. Something deep inside Charles relaxed or perhaps gave up. He would never regain that blithe confidence that he was king of all he surveyed. And he was surprisingly glad of it.

"Are you determined to make trouble?" Robbie's voice broke into his thoughts.

"Not at all. Do tell me, does young Samuel snap his fingers when servants don't move quickly enough to do his bidding?"

"How did you know?"

"He reminds me of someone I used to know."

Robbie thumped into the chair next to him. Charles wished he could pull poor Robbie into his arms and comfort him. Still, the glare he directed at Charles was silly.

Charles said, "My friend, you've already lied to me today. Don't try to convince me you and young Samuel are the best of friends and I've blundered and caused irreparable harm to that friendship."

Robbie growled. "No, of course not. But perhaps Uncle Phillip wished to broach the subject of Samuel's future with his son. It wasn't your place to do so."

"Perhaps." Charles shrugged. "Do you suppose it's a surprise to Samuel that he was to take your place?"

"No." Robbie stretched one of his legs in front of him, slumped down in his seat and rested his folded hands on his flat stomach, a position far more informal, and defeated, than his usual posture. "And so I must beg your pardon. Of course Samuel knows or must strongly suspect his father's plans."

"Why were you so upset?"

It was Robbie's turn to shrug. He propped his elbow on the mahogany table and rested his chin on his hand. At least he'd lost the angry twist to his mouth.

Charles waved a hand to catch his attention.

Robbie almost smiled. "Go on, you must have theories. I'm sure you're eager to tell me." His eyes had regained the light of patience and humor.

Charles considered lying, but, even if he might drive off his one friend, he'd lost patience with dissembling. "I expect you're upset because your uncle probably discussed the situation with your cousin but not with you. It's difficult to feel vital and needed when you're not consulted about your own position." More harping upon the theme of humiliation, he thought.

"It hardly matters why I was upset. I'm not anymore. I am master of my emotions."

"I can see that."

"Yes, and I hope you respect my position on the matter." Robbie gave him a crooked smile. "*Lord,* as my cousin would say. Forgive me. I'm rude again. It's just that I don't like what you said just before Samuel came into the room..."

"I'd accused you of wanting me." Charles leaned close. "We hadn't gotten to the other half of that interesting conversation. I want you too. Very much. I want to hold you and kiss you and do unspeakably obscene and wonderful things with you."

Robbie jumped up quickly and backed away as if Charles held a knife or had transformed into a poisonous snake. He breathed hard. "Please. Don't do that, Charles."

"All right." Charles leaned back in his chair. He wanted to call Robbie a coward, but that was unfair. He'd give his friend time to absorb the idea, sleep on it—or lose sleep over it.

"You are smiling at me," Robbie accused.

"I like you."

"Good heavens. You've said as much in a most unseem—"

Charles interrupted, "'I want you' and 'I like you' are two different statements, Robbie. Both happen to be true. You told me to shut up about the one only. Do you want me to stay silent about our friendship as well?"

A small smile quirked Robbie's mouth but only for a moment. "Of course not. Despite my best judgment, I like you too."

Charles felt absurdly pleased. "You want me as well, but I promise not to mention that again."

"No you shouldn't talk—"

"Robbie! Didn't you hear me? I *won't* mention it. Any further conversation on the subject will be up to you, my friend. I won't turn you into a victim of my lust. Or yours," he added, because honestly, watching Robbie squirm was amusing.

"Worthington," he groaned.

"Yes?" Charles adopted the attitude of eager innocence. That manner worked so well when Robbie employed it.

"You're... Never mind." Robbie sat again and folded his arms tight over his chest. "Please. I ask you as a friend. Leave off. It's—it hurts."

"Why?"

"I owe everything to Uncle Phillip. Without his aid, I might have ended up in a foundling home. He didn't have to claim me, but he did. And you and I both know that any sort of inappropriate affection between us would pain him deeply. Do not ask me to indulge in anything that would insult my uncle. Especially while I live under his roof and eat his food."

The quiet dignity of his answer—as well as his honesty—made Charles swallow his sniping comment about prudishness. "Alas. I'm right on all counts. Although it hardly gives me any sense of satisfaction to know I'm not the only one to suffer from unrequited...er...lust."

Robbie opened his mouth but then just shook his head.

"Yes, I know you're fed to the eyeteeth with this conversation, but it's important to have it out in the open."

"Why? Why do we need to talk about something that will never happen and that my family finds despicable?"

"At least you didn't include yourself in that phrase about 'despicable'. I'm glad you're not one of those dreary men who hate their desires. You're a plucky soul, dear Robbie."

"I don't have any reason to love that part of myself. I would much prefer to want something better." Charles heard the unspoken part of the statement: *I wished I desired women.*

"Yes, and you want to dance and fence too, my poor friend." For the first time in quite a long while, Charles felt pity for someone other than himself. "But as you said yesterday or perhaps the day before, some things must be borne, and if we carry that weight, we might as well do so cheerfully. And now we both are aware of an extra burden we each carry."

"About each other," Robbie muttered, and it was as close to a confession as Charles would hear.

Enough.

He lightly brushed Robbie's knuckles, hiding his surprise created by the heat of the contact. "Truly, I'm done and won't torment you any longer. But baring the truth even for a few minutes is better than pretending it doesn't exist. We will hide it again, see?" He closed his hands into fists and then mimed opening them with the dramatic flourish of a conjuror in a music hall. "Hey presto, and it is gone forever." He couldn't help adding, "Unless you find you wish to say more."

Robbie rolled his eyes. Charles laughed.

He wanted Robbie more than he'd wanted any man in his life, hardly surprising when he reflected that it had been so very long since he'd held anyone. And of course, forbidden pleasures are the ones that tug hardest.

"Shall we go to tea?" Robbie asked.

He was about to answer when the tingling began. "No, oh no."

"Charles? What's wrong?"

Perhaps there was a wrathful god and Charles was being punished for attempting to seduce a good man. The fatigue hit him. Again. The sheer weight rolled over him, almost worse than the tingling fingers, the wave of tiredness so bone-deep he couldn't lift his arm.

This awful symptom had stopped weeks ago. He'd finally beaten many of the imaginary foes in his body, and now the fact that this symptom returned, swooping out of the blue, was enough to make him want to scream and beat his own body to obey him.

If only he hadn't emptied his flask with Forrester. He could drink and deaden the dread.

"Are you upset?" Robbie leaned close. "What's wrong?" He peered into Charles's eyes, so close he looked from one eye to the other. "You're not punishing me with silence, are you?"

"No, no." Charles felt his answer coming from far beyond his own body. "It's nothing."

At least he could speak. At the very worst time, when he thought he might die, his voice had failed him and he'd been trapped, mute, in his own body.

He stared up at Robbie's worried eyes. "I'm fine," he lied.

If his bladder stopped functioning this time, at least he could blame Gemma's little dog.

Indignity.

He knew Robbie wouldn't go away unless he explained. "Sometimes, I have what I call spells."

"Do they last long?"

Charles swallowed. He'd promised himself he wouldn't lie to Robbie. "Well. The longest lasted perhaps four months. But the doctors say it's nothing, or rather it's not really my body's look-out." He pretended to laugh, *ha-ha, it's all absurd,* but his voice had grown thick and emerged peculiar, grating like a rake across gravel.

"That's nonsense. I can see you've changed. Your skin has grown pale. Your eyelids are too heavy. Don't tell me there's nothing wrong with you."

"You believe me." Charles's voice went gruff for a different reason now.

"I believe my own eyes, for pity's sake. And you tell me your symptoms, of course I believe you. There is something physically wrong with you. And I would call a physician, not a nerve specialist, to help you."

"No. There's nothing. Please, go have your tea. Go on."

"I don't want to leave you."

"Thank you for that." Charles blinked. His eyes stung, and he wasn't sure if it was from tears or resumption of the blasted symptoms. He wanted to escape into sleep or indulge in frustrated anger, but Robbie wouldn't go away. Frustration and gratitude warred in Charles.

Robbie didn't appear to notice. "We will go together to tea. It is only tea, so you might escape after one cup and, say, a finger sandwich."

"Robbie. It's not a good idea."

The stubborn man had hold of the handles of his chair and pushed him toward the library door. "You'll see, it will be fine."

"Robbie. Damn it!"

He must have heard the desperation in Charles's voice, because he came to a stop and walked around from the back of the chair to stare down at him. Charles said, "At the very worst times, my symptoms included incontinence. I will not, I *can't* allow that. Not in front of witnesses."

That hadn't been so very difficult to admit after all.

"Oh." Robbie drew up a chair and sat across from him again. "I see. And you think that might happen again?"

"How the hell should I know? That particular mortification took place two months, no, at least three months ago. But I know nothing. I thought I'd improved, and now I am all over tingling and in pain."

"You're worried about a total relapse?"

The thought brought a wave of nausea with it, but he managed to respond calmly enough. "I can't predict any of it."

Robbie went to the back of the room, where a single trunk had been stashed under a bookshelf of encyclopedias. He returned with a blanket, which he put over Charles's lap.

"This will disguise any sort of, ah, problem. And if the worst has happened, then send me a signal of some sort, and I'll wheel you back here as if we were running a race."

"A signal. What? Do you want me to whistle? Or perhaps I might employ naval semaphore flags?"

"Speak a phrase. Something only I shall understand."

Charles rubbed his face. His hands still tingled worse than ever, but the strange fatigue had lifted somewhat. He shook his head. "You are a strange man, Grayson. What do you have in mind? How about 'I hear the sunflowers are especially pretty this year'?"

Robbie guffawed. "I left a deck of cards in my trunk?"

"Mr. Grayson, I am partial to purple flowers."

"I should like to see a rabbit." Robbie's laughter made it difficult to understand him, and it was utterly contagious.

"Is that a rooster I hear crowing?"

By the time they'd stopped laughing at their own absurdities—wiping their eyes and still erupting with occasional chuckles—Charles had forgotten his fear of the creeping, silent illness with no name. Or rather, he hadn't forgotten it; his body wouldn't allow that. He'd simply let go of the fear again. Robbie Grayson wouldn't allow him to hang on to it.

This man was good for him in so many ways. He challenged and offered friendship and encouragement. Charles simply couldn't do without him. And then it really struck him that, with Samuel back, Robbie would be leaving, maybe not in the next few days but surely within a month. What would he do without the presence of this kind, witty man? Charles couldn't believe he'd initially written Robbie off as a nonentity. The man was absolutely vital—at least to him, and he couldn't stomach the idea of convalescence without Robbie beside him.

All the more reason to fight against his mysterious debilitating illness while he still had Robbie to help him.

"All right, then. *Forward the Light Brigade. Charge for the guns,*" Charles quoted.

And his good friend took hold of the wheelchair and pushed him in to tea.

Chapter Seven

Tea was usually an informal meal in the drawing room, but today they gathered at the dining table that was laid with the best china and the finest lacy linens in honor of Samuel's return. Lenore had put on a rose gown with even more ruffles and gathers and tucks than usual. Her gold-and-garnet earrings clashed with the pink, but her wide smile made up for any fashionable shortcomings.

Bertie had been allowed to attend tea but he'd been stuffed into a light blue velvet sailor suit several years too young for him. Red-cheeked and scowling, he met Robbie's eye with such a look of horrified anger that Robbie wanted to laugh—and soothe the poor boy.

"So delightful to have you home again, my darling." Aunt Lenore reiterated the refrain to her son for perhaps the sixth time since they'd sat down to tea. She reached out to pat Samuel's hand. "I'm pleased you came home early. I was not at all comfortable with the idea of you gallivanting around Europe with that fast crowd."

Samuel pulled away, his irritation evident. "They're not 'fast', Mother. They're simply not the parochial types you're used to. My friends from university are educated, worldly and clever. They're not bumpkins."

"They're also spoiled sots, relying on family names and fortunes to carry them through life," Uncle Phillip chimed in. "These are not the young men I would wish you to emulate, Samuel."

"No. You would wish me to be more like our beloved Cousin Robbie." Samuel made his name a sneer, and Robbie took this cue to push back his chair and stand. Let father and son have it out without an audience.

"Mr. Worthington, you seem as if you could use a rest," he said to Charles. "Shall I accompany you back to your room?"

"You mean the library," Samuel muttered, but no one bothered to respond.

"Yes, please." The fact that two words were all the talkative Charles could manage alerted Robbie to his exhausted state. Throughout tea, he'd monitored Charles's color, his breathing and the long pauses in his speech. Now, he felt the invalid had reached his limit.

By the time he'd helped Charles use the lavatory, an intimate act from which Robbie averted his eyes, and gotten him tucked into bed, the man's complexion was paper white.

"Shall I send someone for the doctor? You appear quite ill." Robbie rested his hand on his cool forehead. No fever, then, but Charles's skin was clammy to the touch.

"No. I just need rest. Sleep. There's nothing a doctor can do. Believe me. I've been examined by the best of them."

Thick eyelashes brushed the man's pale cheeks. Robbie noted that his lashes were nearly as coppery as his hair, and a sprinkling of freckles stood out in sharp relief across his nose.

"All right, then." Robbie stroked locks of hair away from that high brow, then smoothed his hand over Charles's head for a moment. He remembered how nice a soothing hand could feel when one was ill. But he quickly ended his touch as it aroused feelings in him he was doing his damndest to squelch.

Robbie left the dim room and went to check in with Mr. Todd. The bailiff was about to visit some tenants who were in arrears. Robbie offered to check on some late-season fields due for harvesting.

Uncle Phillip entered the office just then. "Put it off until tomorrow. And take Samuel with you, if you can find the lad. I know you'll have more patience educating him about his duties than I would."

Robbie wanted to say he wasn't so sure about that, but he bit his tongue.

And so the next morning after breakfast, he located Samuel lounging on a stone bench in the garden, smoking a cheroot and blowing rings through the low-hanging branches of an ornamental cherry tree, much to the delight of Gemma and Bertie.

"Let me try," Bertie begged. "Show me how, and I'm sure I can do it too."

"Afraid not, *mon frère*. Smoking is a bit beyond your years," Samuel drawled. It seemed he drawled everything these days in an affected tone Robbie found utterly annoying.

Gemma spotted Robbie and ran down the flagstone path to cling to his hand and lead him toward the bench. "Samuel's back to stay. Isn't that lovely? And he can blow smoke rings!"

"So I see. A clever skill to learn at university." Robbie forced a smile. "It's good to have your brother home, isn't it? But I'm afraid I must take Samuel away for a little while." He addressed his oldest cousin. "Your father asked me to take you along to the north fields with me. We're to see how harvesting is going for Mr. Fulbright."

"Farmer Not-so-bright is still alive?" Samuel exclaimed. "He must be a hundred and ten years old."

"Fulbright junior, not senior," Robbie corrected. "So, if you'll change into something less formal..."

"Let's hope Junior is a more competent man than his pater. If not, perhaps it's time to replace them with tenants who can turn a profit."

For a young man who hadn't been around the place in years other than holidays, Samuel had strong opinions. Robbie didn't bother to respond that the Fulbrights had occupied their bit of land for nearly as long as the Chesters had been their landlords. One didn't just casually remove tenants.

Robbie stood by, arms folded, waiting while Samuel took his time stubbing out his slim cigar and putting the holder away in his smoking pouch, all the while chatting with his eager younger brother. It was obvious Bert idolized his sophisticated brother, and Robbie prayed again that the little lad wouldn't follow in Samuel's patent leather footsteps.

It took nearly another forty minutes for Samuel to change into what he dubbed "work attire", even though the boots were polished to a reflecting shine and his jacket was a fine woolen one. At last, the two men mounted a pair of chestnut horses outside the stable and headed across country to the Fulbrights'.

Robbie had never sat easily in the saddle, though he muddled through. Samuel, on the other hand, rode erect and elegant. Robbie couldn't help but admire his cousin's athleticism as he always had. He pushed away his slight jealousy. So Samuel was a fine physical specimen. At least Robbie had a head for business.

They approached the fields of barley, where threshing machines pulled by horses were slowly cutting their way along the rows. Robbie reined in and simply appreciated the sight of the rippling golden grain under an achingly blue sky, and the men toiling to bring in the crop. So simple and elemental, and yet so beautiful.

"Lord, it truly is dreary here, isn't it?" Samuel exclaimed. "I don't know how I shall be able to stand it."

Robbie looked toward him, taken aback by the statement. "I thought you would be eager to take the reins from your father. I thought running the estate was what you wanted."

"*Owning* the estate is what I want. But, really, can't that Mr. Todd take care of the day-to-day on his own? Isn't that why we hire a bailiff? I can't be expected to live out here in the middle of nowhere all year round, can I? Everyone I know spends the Season in London. It's the way most civilized gentlemen behave, but not my father. He fancies himself a man of the land year round. He's a simpleton."

Robbie was struck speechless. Last time he'd talked to Samuel, his cousin had made it clear he resented Robbie for acting as his father's right hand. Now that the prime spot was his for the taking, he didn't want it? What was the matter with that spinning weathercock?

Nonplussed, Robbie changed the subject. "There's Mr. Fulbright." He pointed out the farmer laboring with the threshing team. "His father died only a few months ago, so you might remember to offer your condolences."

Robbie dismounted and tied his horse to a fencepost, then made his way across the rough ground and broken stalks, his cane poking holes in the loose earth. He had to concentrate to keep his balance, and when he looked up, Samuel had passed him and was already speaking to Fulbright.

"So sorry to hear about your father's passing, my good man. Tragic loss. How are you bearing up?" Samuel clapped a hand on the farmer's shoulder.

"Well enough." Fulbright pulled out a red handkerchief and wiped his face. He darted a questioning glance at Robbie as if asking who Samuel was. He apparently didn't recognize the rarely seen elder son of the house.

"Mr. Fulbright, you remember Mr. Samuel Chester. He'll soon be helping in the management of the estate."

Fulbright tucked away the cloth into his trousers pocket and nodded. "Ah, young Master Samuel. It's good to see you home."

"How's the harvest coming along?" Samuel stooped to pick up a shorn head of barley and studied it as if he knew good grain from bad.

"Well enough." Fulbright repeated his stock answer.

Robbie pulled out his small notebook and asked the farmer a few questions about the yield per acre and the quality of the grain. He took notes and estimated the profit if the barley sold at current market price, carefully writing the estimates in the book to show Mr. Todd later.

"Indeed, it is a good season." Robbie glanced up at the blue sky. "And you've beaten the rain they say is coming. Well done."

Fulbright cast a glance at the harvesters, and it was clear he was eager to get back to work, so Robbie bid him good day and headed toward his grazing horse.

"That's it? We rode all the way out here to ask a few questions?" Samuel said.

"That and to make the family's presence felt. It's important the farmers understand the Chesters are on their team, so to speak, invested in their success." Robbie hauled himself into the saddle with a grunt and some squirming, wishing he could perform the task more gracefully, particularly in front of Samuel. "Anyway, it's a lovely day for a ride."

"I suppose there's little else to do here," Samuel agreed glumly.

They were in sight of the familiar gables and dormers of the family homestead before Samuel spoke again. He'd been riding in front of Robbie, but now he dropped back to trot beside him. "I say, how about a bit of entertainment tonight?"

"What did you have in mind?" Robbie couldn't begin to think what an exuberant young man like Samuel might find entertaining here. Somehow he doubted a game of Snap with Gemma would satisfy him.

"After dinner, we'll go to the pub and rub elbows with the locals. You can reintroduce me around. If I'm eventually to become squire, I suppose I ought to at least have a refresher course on all the names and families in the district."

Robbie couldn't think of anything he'd less rather do than spend an entire evening in his cousin's company when Samuel was in this sort of mood, but Samuel seemed to be trying to fulfill his purpose here, which was a good thing. "All right."

"We'll bring that poor cripple along. He must be bored out of his mind after being cooped up here for days. I understand Worthington was quite the gay blade prior to his accident, the sort who's the life of any party. I'm sure he misses that social whirl. We'll give him a good airing out."

Gay blade. Life of the party. Robbie was taken aback at hearing Samuel talk about Charles that way. Not to mention "airing out" made him sound as if Charles was a set of musty sheets. He'd come to think of Charles as *his* personal friend, and as someone like himself who enjoyed quieter pursuits such as an evening spent reading. He'd almost forgotten that Charles had lived a full social life before he came to the Chesters. If he had the opportunity, no doubt he'd return to that "social whirl". Charles's friendship and even his attraction to Robbie were very temporary—an important thing to remember.

"He's in a wheelchair," Robbie pointed out.

"We'll have the footmen load him into the carriage at our end, and some beefy farmers can carry him into the pub." Samuel blithely solved the problem.

"I suppose we could ask him," Robbie said uncertainly.

"We can and we shall. *Lord,* don't worry, Cousin, a merry time will be had by all."

Loaded onto the back of the open pony cart like so much luggage, jolted over rough roads, then carried into the local brewing establishment and plunked onto a chair. Charles wanted nothing more than to drink himself flat. How far he had fallen. His dignity was nonexistent, and fear of another attack of the debilitating tingles loomed over him.

The yeasty smell of hops was rich in the air and soaked into the very patina of the wood floor in the dimly lit pub. Charles had expected Samuel to go through to the saloon bar, but they settled in the public room. Men with slouched shoulders, their elbows on tables, hunkered over large glasses of ale. A soft muttering of voices and the clink of glasses against wood made a companionable, familiar sound that soothed Charles's spirit. This was the first time he'd been outside the house and gardens of the Chester estate since he'd arrived. It felt good to see other places and other people, though he didn't care for everyone staring back at him.

He'd missed Robbie far too much today. The thought of his friend roaming the countryside on horseback had made Charles impatient and filled with ridiculous longing. He wanted ride next to Robbie, breathing the sweet, dusty air of late summer. Once he recovered from that bout of self-pity, he decided the best thing to do was attempt to strengthen his weakened body with exercise.

He'd practiced standing on his own, falling back onto the bed over and over, and ended frustrated and trembling. When Stewart at last showed up to announce lunch, he'd begged off, pleading a headache. That was certainly true enough, and he wasn't sure he could face his relations without the buffer of Robbie.

Now he had to share Robbie with the insufferable Samuel. Ah well, at least he'd had a glimpse of the evening sky, and now he could stare at something other than the walls of that library.

Anyway, he'd made a promise to himself not to overimbibe, so he would go easy on the ale tonight.

They'd set him in a chair with padding and arms, a bit better than most of the plain wood chairs and benches that surrounded the tables of this public house. The place was dim, dingy and older than the hills, but quaint in a country sort of way.

The rafters near the fireplace were dark with the smoke of decades. The flagstone floor had probably been covered with reeds not so very long ago but was now swept fairly clean. The windows with the tiny diamond panes of wrinkled glass probably hadn't been cleaned since the last century.

The publican brought the first round of drinks directly to their table, a gesture of honor for members of one of the best families in the district. The old man's face was seamed with wrinkles, and veins traced his cheeks and his purple nose. A habitual drinker, unsurprising given his livelihood.

"Welcome," he greeted them. "Good to have you back, Master Samuel."

"You'll likely see a lot of me now, Mister…"

"Green," Robbie supplied.

"Oh right. Mr. Green. I do recall. Go ahead and chalk it on the slate, my good man."

The welcoming smile on Green's face dimmed. "Yes, sir."

Charles knew that look. He'd seen it on the face of his tailor, his barber, and many other tradesmen, who feared giving offense to a superior even more than they feared running a line of credit. Eventually those faces had grown harder and the demands for money more urgent. Only when lawsuits threatened had Charles come to the realization that his old life was truly over.

"Well, gents. Here we are. Drink up." Samuel's bonhomie was as thin as tissue paper and nearly as transparent. Charles wasn't quite certain why the young man, who clearly resented both of them, had dragged them to the alehouse with him, but he guessed it had much to do with Samuel dreading quietness and the opportunity to look into his own soul.

Such deep and maudlin thoughts for so early in the evening and after only a few sips of beer, yet Charles couldn't help but continue to see his old self reflected in young Samuel Chester. Drinking, carousing, gambling and any sort of diversion had always been preferable to time spent alone. But now he didn't mind solitude nearly as much. He'd come to terms with it. And it was much easier with Robbie there to talk to. Quiet evenings were pleasant at last. He'd never have guessed that playing cards with Gemma and Bertie would be preferable to, say, going to the races with his friends. If he were healthy and wealthy again and able to pursue livelier activities, Charles realized he was no longer much interested in them.

After about fifteen minutes of monologue about his friends and their adventures in Europe, Samuel interrupted his own chatter. "Lord, but you two are gloomy! We're here to have fun. Do you know any jokes or bawdy stories, anything to pass the time?"

Charles met Robbie's gaze over the rim of the glass Robbie drank from—another deep draught, Charles noticed. Robbie rolled his eyes, and Charles smiled.

"Yes. I have a tale. Stop me if you've heard this one," Charles began.

Just then the door of the crowded Rye and Oats opened, and a party of young people came into the pub along with a blast of cool air. Several gentlemen were accompanied by a couple of brightly dressed ladies who appeared very fun-loving and more than a little drunk already. Boisterous voices and loud laughter proclaimed their presence.

"Isn't that Jarrod Watersmith?" Samuel asked, nodding toward a young man with extremely wide lapels and a garish green-and-yellow-striped waistcoat. "I do believe it is." He lifted his hand and half rose from his seat. "Smithy, could that be you? It's been dogs' years since I've seen you."

"Jarrod Watersmith?" Charles asked Robbie.

Robbie shrugged and set down his empty glass. "Another land-owning family in the district. They run mostly sheep. The family hasn't been here as long as the Chesters, but they're certainly well established." He squinted at the group. "I believe the other men must be visiting friends, and the ladies..."

"Ah, the ladies I believe I recognize," Charles said archly. "They're the sort who hover around rich young gentlemen, hoping for a leg up in the world."

Robbie frowned and squinted harder before leaning toward Charles. "Pros-itutes?"

Sour mash scented his breath. Drunk, off one tall glass of ale? Charles smiled and shook his head.

"Maybe not quite, but certainly women of easy virtue."

Robbie seemed to study the fancy-dressed escorts, who bloomed like fresh flowers in the purely masculine pub.

Around the big room came soft mutters about forward women and the lack of a ladies' bar in the small pub, but no one demanded the ladies leave.

Samuel leaped out of his seat and was across the room in three strides, greeting his boyhood friend. He spoke loud enough that Charles and Robbie could clearly hear him. "Odd we haven't run across each other before now, seeing as we occupy the same circles."

"I spent some time in New York with relatives." Watersmith spoke with a world-weary drawl even more affected than Samuel's. His auburn hair lay in artfully tousled curls, no doubt made wilder at the hands of one of the young ladies in the group. He studied Samuel with keen eyes, as if assessing what, if any, value his old acquaintance might have. Charles

88

recognized that look. He was sure he'd worn it himself as a younger man. If Watersmith deemed Samuel less than up to snuff, he'd cut off the conversation, but if he thought Samuel might fit in with his crowd, he'd bring him along. "Quite a different world across the puddle. I highly recommend it. Do catch me up on what you've been doing."

"I graduated and toured Europe. You simply must go."

Samuel pulled up a chair at the table of fun, lively youths without ever looking back at his relations.

"Well, there's dear Samuel lost to us." Charles shifted in his seat, trying to find a more comfortable position. "Appears he's found greener pastures with the shepherd's son."

"Well, the Watersmiths don't actually *tend* the sheep. They only own the land." Robbie spoke as seriously as a parson. The little furrow between his brows was adorable and Charles abruptly wanted to kiss it—kiss tipsy Robbie right there on his forehead.

Robbie lifted a hand, hailing the server to ask for another drink.

"Do you feel maybe you've had enough?" Charles asked, utterly aware at the irony of *him* being the one to worry about quantities of alcohol imbibed in.

"It tastes quite good. Very quenching," Robbie said. "It's been a long time since I've had anything other than a glass of wine or port to drink."

"It's fairly potent beer," Charles warned.

"Yes. Rich and dark and with an interesting aftertaste." Robbie held the glass of ale up to the light and studied it intently.

"Oh, my friend, you are going to have a big head on you come morning."

Robbie looked at him. "Big head?"

"A morning-after headache," Charles explained. "You're not used to drinking at all."

"Nonsense. I'm fine." Robbie slurred his esses like a music hall parody of a drunk.

"Perhaps we should leave after you finish your drink. I hardly think Samuel will mind if he's left to find his own way home."

They both looked over to the table where uproarious laughter erupted. One of the girls had sidled up close to Samuel and was whispering in his ear.

"No, I don't think Samuel will miss us at all," Robbie agreed. "Whoo. I feel a little woozy. I suppose I wouldn't mind some fresh air. I'll get someone to help transport you to the cart and tell Shmamual...tell my cousin what we're about."

He rose from his chair, swayed for a second and touched the edge of the table to steady himself, then Robbie moved with slow, stately steps across the room, relying heavily on his cane to keep him upright.

It took him a moment to get Samuel's attention. The young man was much more interested in what the pretty blonde had to say than in listening to his dreary cousin. At last he turned to Robbie with an expression of exasperation.

The din of voices in the pub had grown so loud that Charles couldn't hear the exchange, but a wave of Samuel's hand let him know they were cavalierly dismissed. Good! He'd had more than enough of the boy's company for one evening.

It galled him that he couldn't stand and walk to the cart under his own steam. Waiting to be carried like an infant was excruciating. Charles finished off his glass of India Pale Ale. A drop in the bucket, not remotely enough to fog his senses—unlike Robbie, who weaved his way back to Charles with a couple of hefty young lads in tow.

In short order, they'd laced their hands and lifted him up, with an arm around their shoulders. The night breeze was a slap in the face after the overheated pub. Charles felt every sense alive with awareness as he settled onto the front seat of the pony trap beside Robbie.

After thanking the young men, Robbie took the reins and clucked at the little pony to move it forward. The cart rattled over cobblestones in town and a rutted dirt road once they reached the village limits. Charles clung to the edge of the bench as the cart jostled over a particularly deep pit, sliding him even closer to Robbie. Their hips and thighs pressed together warmly.

Charles glanced at Robbie's profile, the high-bridged nose and strong chin, eyes on the road before them. They were alone out here on the country road. Completely alone, without any chance of a servant or cousin or anyone else interrupting them. It was all Charles could do not to put his hand on Robbie's thigh, just to check his reaction. But he'd promised he wouldn't push beyond friendship—not unless invited.

Overhead, brilliant stars glittered in a velvet sky and a nearly full moon rose above the trees. Charles tipped his head back to study the stars, so beautiful and aloof and far above human weaknesses and tragedies, hopes and fears. He tilted his chin back down to say something along those lines to Robbie, only to find Robbie staring at him.

He dropped the reins into his lap, giving the pony its head. The animal continued to plod forward while Robbie reached out, grasped the back of Charles's neck and dragged him in for a kiss.

Charles grunted in surprise. Explosions went off inside him. His lips burned. It was as if he'd never been kissed before, and it wasn't as though Robbie had some great technique. His lips were a bit dry, his mouth closed and mashed bruisingly against Charles's mouth, but the *fact* of that kiss, the desperate passion behind it, was thrilling.

He'd dreamed of this for days but had begun to realize nothing was actually going to happen between them. Now here it was Robbie who'd gone berserk and was attacking him with kisses and holding him so tightly he could hardly breathe. Astonishing and wonderful what a glass or two of ale could do!

But Charles didn't want to take advantage of Robbie's drunken state. He would hate regrets to arise the next morning and possibly ruin their friendship. Charles took Robbie by the shoulders and gently pushed him back.

"Do you know what you're doing? Are you sure?" He looked into lust-glazed eyes that glittered in the moonlight.

"Yes." Robbie exhaled the word on a sigh. "Yes, I'm absolutely sure. I'm not *that* inebriated. I know what I want."

Charles assessed Robbie's commitment and level of tipsiness before nodding. "All right, then. Why don't you pull this cart onto some quiet lane off the main road where there's no chance of anyone passing by."

"And then we can kiss some more?"

Charles smiled. "Then we can kiss *and* more."

Chapter Eight

Only a few splotches of moonlight penetrated the dark grove Robbie chose. He tied the pony to a sapling, then climbed back up to Charles and more kisses. Their hats ended up in the cart. Their ties and collars soon joined the hats. The cob dozed in its traces.

No boundaries lay between Robbie and astounding pleasure.

Beautiful night, beautiful kisses, beautiful man in his arms. Euphoria bubbled over inside him as Charles pressed his *beautiful* soft lips against Robbie's. Oh, so this was how it was done. Charles slid his lips softly, lightly over Robbie's. He nibbled. He teased. He coaxed Robbie to open his lips and then, oh! His warm, wet tongue slid inside.

Robbie whimpered with sharp longing. Everything in his past, lascivious, guilty daydreams were nothing compared to this yearning. He had to get closer, touch as much of Charles as he could.

The large hands cupping his head held him steady, but as he moved closer, wrapping his arms around Charles, the dratted fingers grasped his shoulders and pushed him away. He opened his eyes and, in the pale shaft of moonlight, realized Charles regarded him steadily, without the usual smile he aimed at Robbie.

"Robbie. Now I'm remembering too much. Those things you said just yesterday in the library."

Robbie's lips felt chilled without the intoxicating heat of Charles against them. His mind whirled as if he'd drunk a dozen pints of ale. Why in God's name was Charles talking when they should be kissing? Words abandoned him. He gave a small noise, a mix of protest and confusion, instead. "Hrm?"

Charles explained, "When I informed you that we would eventually come together, you appealed to my better self. You pointed out that you respect Phillip."

"I do." Robbie nodded.

"That respect meant following his rules under his roof," Charles said.

A loophole. "We aren't under his roof."

"Is it that simple? I like you, Robbie, don't forget. I won't have you blaming yourself or me if you should end up with a wagonload of guilt. It has to be more than the beer speaking."

"More than the beer speaking?" he repeated. Was that an expression he knew?

Charles said, "Ah, perhaps I've had a bit too much to drink as well. When alcohol is running through one's system, it can make one abandon long-held principles."

Robbie felt the rise and fall of Charles's chest. A sigh. He went on, speaking slowly as if feeling his way through a novel thought. Robbie knew that sensation. He'd experienced it frequently since Charles had come to the hall—bombshells of emotion and beliefs, new and frightening and burning through his old notions.

He'd been blown up by his new friend. Now he needed Charles to put Robbie back together—more of those kisses and embraces would do the trick nicely. Less thinking. More action.

But Charles was still speaking, and he must pay attention. "If you avoided me after...after we indulged, I would be extremely—I would be bereft. Losing you as a friend would

make me sadder than missing the chance for some embraces."
He sounded astounded by his own thinking.

"Ha! We are good friends, Mr. Worthington. I know that.
Such good, close friends, but I think closer would be better." He
stroked his hand over Charles's cheek, and ran his fingers
through the thick, soft hair. Mm. He wanted to feel that hair
against his mouth, perhaps taste the skin at his temple and
throat, but dammit, Charles still gripped his shoulders.

"You contradict yourself."

"Yes, I do." Robbie laughed. "Every day is a giant
hodgepodge of contradictions in my heart and brain when it
comes to you. But see? It's night, not day. We're not under my
uncle's roof, and it is dark, and no one will know. If I have any
regrets tomorrow, they will be mine alone, and I won't blame
you." He reached into his waistcoat pocket and pulled out the
small leather-bound notebook he carried, along with the nub of
a pencil. "See? I shall write this down right next to my
estimations of the barley crop." He flipped open the small book,
such a familiar action, licked the end of the pencil, and began
to write.

"I am an adult." He read the words he couldn't see in the
dark as he scrawled them in his book. "Anything I do tonight or
any other night or day is my own look-out. No one else can be
blamed for my actions, including my good, dear friend, Mr.
Charles Worthington. Tonight I will concentrate only on desire.
Signed, Robert Grayson."

"I had no notion you were capable of such silliness."
Charles's smile warmed his voice.

"I had no idea either. I think it's good for me." Robbie
suddenly felt solemn as he tucked book and pencil away.
Somehow, saying and writing those words felt as if he'd evoked
a genuine pledge. "Casting away concerns just for tonight, just
for now—that will be good. I don't think I have ever purposefully
abandoned duty. Another fresh experience thanks to you."

"Yes, this is new for me as well."

"You? You are a man of the world. You know all about pleasure. You have kissed hundreds of men and touched them too." The thought of this made his breath come faster. Charles would use those clever, experienced hands on him. *Now. Soon.*

"Hardly hundreds. The new experience is that I'm forced to worry about my partner."

Robbie patted the notebook in his waistcoat. "I'm not your concern, see? We're done with talking, damn you."

"What would you like to do instead?" That warm, teasing tone would undo him.

"No talking, no thinking—that leaves only feeling. I want to touch every inch of you. I wish we could undress and be naked, but not here."

"No," agreed Charles. The single word was a growl.

"But I shall touch you," Robbie warned. "As much of you as I can."

"I hardly recognize you, Robbie."

"I don't recognize myself. Come here. Oh, pardon. I forgot." He must go to Charles, whose legs didn't work, but then there was a creak and a shift, and Charles had moved close. He grabbed Robbie and hauled him onto his lap.

Robbie leaned into a kiss and, yes, his hungry fingers found that warm hair, the unshaved skin and those impossibly wide, muscular shoulders.

Charles's arms surrounded him, a shelter and the storm in the same locked embrace.

The kisses turned slow again, gentle and exploratory. But Robbie's restlessness returned. He needed to move, and he must discover all of Charles. Hands weren't enough. His body from his head to his cock to his thighs, hell, his toes, ached to touch Charles. He clutched Charles's jacket and twisted.

Placing his knees on the bench, Robbie spread his thighs wide to accommodate the large body under him.

Now he was the taller of them and bent his head to taste Charles while he pushed, demanding and hot, against Charles's torso and, ah, yes, that lovely hard tree branch of a cock.

The breath hissed from Robbie's mouth as he rubbed his prick against Charles. Too much cloth separated them. He reached down and unbuttoned their flies. He drew out the tails of their shirts, pushed them up, unbuttoned their waistcoats. Several square inches of uncovered skin lay within reach. He'd seen Charles's body while he cared for him, and had imagined exploring the texture of the firm muscle and the hair on this belly. The reality left the fantasy behind. And then, rising up to meet the skin of his belly, was that magnificent cock.

"Oh God." Charles moaned as Robbie fumbled at their trousers, their drawers. Charles placed his hands on Robbie's shoulders again, clutching him in an almost ceremonial position as if refusing to take part in this debauchery—even as his hips arched up.

Robbie used both hands tucked between their bodies to grip their cocks, Charles's almost extravagantly large and round-headed, and his own, not as large but so hard for Charles, already slick and harder than he'd ever been in his life. This was excitement defined.

His balls ached for release, but he wouldn't allow this rare pleasure to end. He wrapped both hands around Charles and explored the heat and the iron and the lovely slide of him. The hands on his shoulders squeezed almost too tightly.

"Robbie, God. Oh." The sound of Charles's groans and heavy, uneven breaths filled the night air.

Charles still gripped him, but Robbie pushed forward so he could rest his head on that broad shoulder, and kiss and lick the salt of his throat as he experimented with the hot iron bar of flesh in his hands, the soft hair at its base.

The ecstasy of all that skin and solid muscle for him. He could finally do what he wanted, touch and taste and kiss, barely drawing enough air as the feverish excitement gripped him.

The crisis of orgasm grew too close, and he clumsily opened his hands so he could clutch them both, slippery skin to skin. Both men groaned as their erections clashed and slid.

Charles's front, naked and open to him—the thought was enough to send Robbie to a climax—but the touch, that was more than enough to push his pleasure into something almost too strong to bear. His head went light, and he nearly blacked out.

Charles's hands supported him then, wrapping tightly around him and hauling him close. Charles hadn't erupted yet. Robbie could feel the restless tension coiled in his lover's body and the erection that still throbbed against his own uncovered belly.

"Let me," he whispered.

Charles only gave a soft, throaty grunt of refusal. His hand wedged between them, and Robbie thrilled to the understanding that the knuckles sliding up and down, brushing him, were bringing the ultimate pleasure. This was what Charles did when alone with his desire. Touching him had been unbearably erotic. The ripple of charged awareness now was almost as arousing.

"You're going to climax soon," he murmured against Charles's neck, where he could feel the fast pulse beat under his lips and hear the gasping breath. He reached down and covered Charles's hand with his, to feel the strength, the speed and grip. Next time it would be his hand alone and maybe his mouth.

Charles shuddered and pushed up. Robbie felt the splash of heat of the superb member as it spent. He pushed his mouth to Charles's neck and kissed him because he wanted to tell him how much he adored this, and he never wanted to give it up. He had never in all his years felt even a shadow of this richness. He couldn't babble those words, not to the worldly Charles. Instead, he buried his nose in at the crook of Charles's neck and held on tight until at last, Charles gently guided him off his lap to sit on the bench again. Robbie had grown sober in these minutes but was still giddy with the new experience.

Chapter Nine

Charles used his handkerchief to wipe himself off. The incident, a bit of groping and awkward frottage, would once have struck him as nothing spectacular. The whole thing from kiss to finish took less than fifteen minutes. A real treat would be Robbie, naked on a wide bed, some delicious oils and several long hours of privacy. He grinned into the night as he shoved his shirt back into his trousers and buttoned himself up.

But he fooled himself to call this mere fumbling. What they'd just done together had been glorious. The fast and furious session, uncertain groping and all, had been quite his most erotic encounter for years. His previous high point, his first surprisingly educational session with the flexible Paul Martin, might even be eclipsed. Hunger, he reflected, made the bread taste like a feast.

Or perhaps it was Robbie's avid response that had made it memorable. Who would have guessed that the quiet young man would turn into a lithe animal? And with such an ability to use simple words to set a man on fire. All right. Charles might have guessed all that, thought about that, imagined that for days now. Yes, hunger and anticipation and a lewd imagination given too much time to dwell on details—those gathered together to turn what might have been a grubby little encounter into the stuff of dreams.

"Are you all right?" Robbie, sitting next to him now, pressed him from shoulder to hip.

"Never better, my Robbit."

"No, I say. Why have you invented that odious nickname?"

"You don't like it?"

"I'm an adult, a man, not a stuffed animal." He sounded amused rather than indignant.

"Mm." Charles stretched and yawned. He resolved to use the name whenever they were alone together. Every bone in his body felt melted and reformed. Not a tightness or tingling disturbed him. "I had no hopes for tonight, but you have made it a most agreeable outing."

"And now? What shall happen now?" Robbie sounded serious and entirely sober.

Charles tried to stifle his impatience, but, by God, he knew this would happen. "Are you feeling regret? Argh, I knew you would regain your damnable conscience and—"

"The only regret I feel is that I can't do that again, now or later or every day for the rest of my life."

That silenced Charles as nothing else could. "You astound me," he said after a full minute of silence. "I thought you'd speak of your obligation to Phillip."

Robbie groaned. "I had managed to forget that topic for a time. But yes, you're right to bring me back to reality." He shuffled on his seat, jumped down and rustled in the bushes.

"Are you doing what I think you are, my proper Robbit? Peeing in the great outdoors?"

"I am a country lad," Robbie said as he climbed back up. "But I was reclaiming the reins. I tied the pony up. Don't call me Robbit."

"Did you? To that tree? I hadn't even noticed." And Robbie was the one who'd had too much to drink this evening. Charles had been too intent on dreaming of kisses.

"One more," he said aloud. "One more kiss for luck before we reclaim the road and return to the hall."

Robbie leaned to him, and their mouths met perfectly for a long, languid and sweet exchange, with heat flaring at the end. Charles pulled away, panting.

"You leave me breathless." He couldn't see Robbie in the darkness but heard his soft laugh.

They didn't speak the rest of the way home. The air was cool and held the scent of growing things and the hint of coming rain. Robbie had to pay careful attention.

A cloud covered the moon, and the dark road was nearly invisible, though the pony apparently knew the way well enough to trot. At last the twinkling lights of the hall became visible.

As they drew close to the gates, Robbie said, "Your chair will be waiting at the side, and I'll take you into bed."

"Wish you could stay there with me."

Robbie didn't say anything, but Charles felt his body stiffen.

"*Pax*, Robbit. Once we enter those gates, the old arrangement stands. No torturing you with attempts at seduction. I'll be thinking of our brief encounter night and day, but I won't attempt to repeat it. That shall be up to you."

"Thank you." Robbie sounded thoroughly sober and himself again.

Had he really succumbed to alcohol or had he needed to pretend he was squiffed to gather the nerve for their encounter? Charles wouldn't accuse him of fakery. He was too grateful for the evening and those kisses. He touched his mouth with his fingers, glad for the slight tenderness created by Robbie's beard. "Thank you," he said. "I feel better than I have..." He stopped to consider. "Than I have for a very, very long time. I feel alive."

"We are through the gates," Robbie reminded him.

"Ha, and perhaps it was the outing, the company in the inn, or the starlight that brought me such enormous...pleasure."

Robbie chuckled.

Charles could undress himself these days, but Robbie had gotten into the habit of standing near to help him should his trousers cause trouble—or perhaps he lingered for other reasons. Now Robbie positioned himself at the far end of the room, with a writing table between them, as if he could flee should Charles make another attempt at seduction.

"Will Samuel be all right, do you suppose?" Charles called over to him.

Robbie rubbed his brow as if trying to recall who exactly Samuel was. "Yes, I hope so. Perhaps I should go tell Uncle Phillip where he is."

"If you carry tales, it will only serve to make the boy's resentment stronger."

The frown deepened as if this obvious point was hard to understand.

"I didn't think of it that way," Robbie said. He came around the table and moved closer. "You're right. I'm used to acting as my uncle's agent."

"You are Samuel's cousin, not his keeper."

"Yes. I'm to keep an eye on him and help him, but I don't suppose that means being his nursemaid." He sat heavily on the chair near Charles's bed. "The trouble is, should he get into trouble, I will at least share the blame."

Charles, who'd managed to strip to his drawers, paused as he pulled on the loose gown he wore at night. "Truly?" he said, astonished.

"Yes, of course."

"It's idiotic. Samuel is no child. Phillip, a strong-willed man with power over the puppy's purse, can't keep him in line. How does he expect you to accomplish the task—you, a cousin Samuel apparently barely heeds?"

The frown returned. "I—I don't know."

"You're wearing the dourest expression. This is not worthy of doom and gloom."

Robbie mastered his features, then slapped his thighs. "Yes, I expect you're right. I shall leave you and go to my own bed."

Robbie, running away again. Obviously he was not interested in discussing the fact that his uncle wasn't a perfect man. The old Charles would have pointed this out, of course, ready to drive home a point no matter the consequences. Being right and self-righteous felt delicious. But Charles knew Robbie and suspected loyalty would drive him to defend the uncle he'd always admired. Better to let him think about this on his own.

"Will you be busy tomorrow too? I missed you today." He winced at his own wheedling tone. "Poor Robbie, pulled in all directions by uncle and invalid."

Robbie looked up then, the ghost of the smile on his face again, his eyes less troubled. "I think I shall be able to help you with your exercises again tomorrow. After all, the sooner you are able to walk, the sooner..." He waved a vague hand.

Yes, the sooner what will happen? The family might reclaim their library? The sooner he might be shuffled off to another branch of the family or perhaps a small cottage on Phillip's lands? A decrepit dependent, waiting for the soup and attention.

Charles bit the inside of his lip sharply to bring him out of these familiar useless thoughts. Then he recalled that the sooner he recovered, the sooner Robbie might move along to something brighter than life at the hall. He'd move to London again, perhaps, or at least Durham, and he would have a chance to discover work he enjoyed and start his real life.

The thought of remaining trapped in this house or village or of removing to another distant cousin's home seemed far less dreary than the thought of losing Robbie forever.

He realized Robbie waited for him to say something. "Yes. The sooner the better," he said at last. "Good night and sleep well, Robbit."

Robbie groaned. "I shall have to think of some odious name for you, Worthlessington."

"Maybe, but *that* is most definitely not a good start."

Robbie moved forward as if he would drop a kiss on Charles's mouth or forehead. Instead he patted his upper arm and picked up the trousers and other clothing Charles, still untrained to life without a manservant, had dropped on the floor. Robbie folded them as if he were a valet, moving gravely as if this was important work. No matter what Robbie did, his employment would never demean him. He would take every task seriously.

Charles had lost any interest in mocking that sort of intensity. Watching that solemn face as Robbie inspected a bit of dirt on the sleeve of a jacket, Charles wished he could make things well and right for his friend. This new desire settled deep within him. It would make a fine replacement for self-pity.

He smiled, and Robbie caught sight of the grin and returned it, that shy, pleased smile Charles tried so hard to coax from him.

God in heaven, he did love that smile. Charles should have been panicked to realize how dearly he held it, but he already had had several moments tonight when he'd been forced to realize how important Robbie had grown. Ah well. Panic and melancholy could wait until Robbie's time at the hall had ended. In the meantime, he'd enjoy the moments they would grab together. He felt confident more kisses lay in his future.

Chapter Ten

Rain drizzled down the windowpanes in long streaks, and the gray gloom outside made the firelight in the parlor all the cheerier. Robbie reached to turn up the flame on the kerosene lamp on top of a nearby end table. Although this room was gaslit, as were all rooms in the old house since the remodel, he needed the extra light cast by the lamp in order to see his work.

Was it work, though? No ledgers and columns full of useful numbers or information. Uncle Phillip would no doubt view Robbie's sketches as a silly hobby. His uncle had never been foursquare behind Robbie's time spent training under M. Richaud. He'd never understood the value of room design. *Buy a carpet, some drapes and a bit of furniture and have done with it,* was his feeling. And yet, though he hadn't been particularly encouraging, Phillip had not stood in Robbie's way back then. Robbie would always be grateful for that.

He dipped pen in ink and sketched a window with lightweight curtains drawn back to emit shafts of light. Every housekeeper knew that light was the enemy of upholstery and carpets. Most parlors were kept dim and shrouded on the sunniest days. Robbie thought that was a way of thinking that needed to be changed. Light should be incorporated into the room, brightening and lifting the spirits of all who entered.

The furniture should be lighter too. Surely the penchant for dark, hulking, over-upholstered pieces must end soon. If he were a designer, he would suggest his clients return to the graceful, airy lines of French provincial, but with a sparer style, fewer curlicues and less gilt.

Robbie sketched a sofa and a cluster of chairs companionably grouped together in that shaft of sunlight. He placed a few *objets d'art* on the fireplace mantel in his room and scribbled a few paintings on the wall—only a few, not stacked on top of each other all the way to the ceiling.

"Less is more," M. Richaud used to say. *"The eye can only observe so many details at once, and a cluttered room is stifling to the soul."*

Of course, Richaud's method of design was old-fashioned and anathema to what most modern citizens considered good taste. But he was slowly making inroads among a few elite and forward-thinking members of society. Eventually the rest must surely follow.

Robbie blew lightly over the ink to make certain it was dry, then turned the page. He measured out the distances—chin to eyes, eyes to hairline—and blocked in the rough approximation of a face. Drawing people was not his forte, but he was accomplished enough, and infatuated enough, to soon produce a fair approximation of the face that haunted him constantly.

Charles Worthington had invaded his life, his mind, and now, even his sketchbook. Robbie added a sparkle to the eyes, twisted up the right corner of the mouth in a mocking smile and added more curl to the hair. He wished he had his watercolors handy so he might try to find the exact shade of mahogany for that hair.

The parlor door opened, and Robbie jumped and snapped the sketchbook closed, likely smearing Charles's image. He turned toward the intruder and saw in living color the very face he'd tried to depict.

Stewart pushed the man's chair, barely making it through the doorframe without scraping. An excited shaking passed through Robbie, but he schooled his face to nonchalance.

"Hoped I might find you here," Charles said. "It's dreadfully dull today, and you didn't stop by to see me this morning."

"I thought I'd... I wanted to work on some..." Robbie floundered, seemingly incapable of completing a sentence. He hoped Stewart didn't notice his discomposure.

"What have you got there? A sketchbook? Let me see."

"No!" Too loud, Robbie realized. "I mean, I don't generally show my sketches to anyone."

"Good heavens, why not? If I had any sort of skill at all, I'd be flaunting it for everyone to see. Park me over there, please, Stewart," Charles commanded.

The footman trudged forward, pushing the chair with difficulty over the carpet and around the array of side tables and ottomans to place him near Robbie's armchair.

"You may leave us," Charles said, with the authoritative tone Robbie noticed he used when addressing servants. Robbie had never learned the knack himself. He could never speak so commandingly to Stewart, or Mrs. Jackson the housekeeper, or even the parlor maid, Lucy.

Once Stewart had closed the door behind him, Charles leaned forward as far as he could and placed a hand on Robbie's knee.

"No. Please don't." Robbie moved his leg away. "Not here."

"Then where, and when? For I definitely need more of you." Charles's eyes glinted exactly as Robbie had drawn them.

Robbie shook his head. "We can't. The other night was... I won't pretend I didn't enjoy it. But we can't repeat what happened. Not ever."

"No. Of course not." Charles grinned.

"I'm quite serious."

"Oh yes, I know." He continued to grin like the Cheshire cat in that children's story. If the rest of the man faded away, his rakish grin would remain, haunting Robbie.

"Stop staring at me like that."

"Like what?"

"As if I were something you wanted to devour." Robbie understood the double meaning and regretted it the moment the words were out of his mouth.

"Ah, my dear Robbit, you can't tease me that way and not expect me to try to kiss you."

"I'm not teasing, damn it." He swallowed and pushed the stopper into his bottle of ink.

"All right, so I'm not to touch you or look at you a certain way. May I at least look at your sketches? Please?"

"I don't... They're not..." Robbie started fumbling again. But he'd made the mistake of setting his book on the arm of the chair, too close to Charles's fast hands. The man grabbed it and began to leaf through.

"Why, these are marvelous. Why on earth wouldn't you want to share them?" He turned another page. "The ones you've painted in particular. The light hues and the delicate lines of the furniture—these are rooms I could imagine living in. Certainly preferable to this monstrous collection. No offence to our dear Lenore but one can have too many Staffordshire figurines."

Charles gestured at the room around them, so profusely packed with pictures and stuffed birds under glass and bone china ornaments that it made one giddy. He bent his head and examined the sketchbook, turning the pages slowly. "This is far better. I wonder how you came to such good taste, living here."

"That's enough. Hand it back, please." Robbie felt quite light-headed and his cheeks burned. "Really. Please."

But it was too late. Charles had reached the portrait of himself. It was a bit smeared from Robbie closing the book while the ink was still damp, but the likeness was clear.

"Oh." Charles looked from the drawing to Robbie. "This is how you see me? I look like a smug, arrogant jackass."

"No. Oh, no." Robbie frowned. "Your smile isn't smug, it's charismatic, and that devilish glint in your eyes—"

"Makes me look the very devil." Charles touched the eyes on the drawing.

"Charms me right out of my senses," Robbie finished. "Everything about you is like...this light." He pointed to the shining, rose-colored globe of the tabletop lamp. "You shine. You make everything around you brighter, more colorful, livelier than it's ever been before. I can't imagine how dark and dreary it would be here without you."

"But it's you who will soon be going away," Charles reminded him. "Back to London perhaps?"

"Or I might settle in Durham. It would be less of an adjustment. And it's closer. Easier to make visits home from there."

"Less opportunity there to pursue this." Charles tapped the sketchbook, which he had mercifully closed. "Your gift is too large for a small city."

Robbie shrugged and didn't say anything more. His rush of words about what Charles meant to him was apparently going to pass unremarked.

But no, he should've known better.

"So, you think I'm a light, eh?" Charles grinned the exact devilish grin that made Robbie's stomach flip. "*Colorful and bright and lively,* I believe? And yet you still think you can withdraw into your shell and pretend that what happened between us is a one-time event? Come now, Robbie. You know better. It's not a matter of 'if' but of 'when'. Somehow we will find time to be together again."

Together. Robbie knew what that meant now. Not merely longing looks or the occasional graze of a hand. They couldn't be content with that any longer. *He* couldn't. Charles was right to think him foolish to believe it.

"All right, then. I will admit that I do want more of *that,* what we did together. But it will certainly not be anywhere in this house." Robbie glanced at the rain streaking the windowpanes. "And we will surely not go riding anyplace today. So for now, we shall just be friends again. A game of chess perhaps?"

Charles sighed deeply and flopped back into his chair. "All right. I've won my point and will concede the match. For today, we will resume being merely friends." He extended his leg and brushed the toe of his shoe up Robbie's calf. Charles winced slightly as if his leg ached, but Robbie was pleased to note he could make this small movement. "Friends who occasionally touch each other," Charles added.

"You are incorrigible. Perhaps you truly are possessed by the devil," Robbie teased, but he didn't move his leg away.

As he clutched his notebook and gathered up his pens, elation and pride filled him. He was glad Charles had seen his work and expressed more than mere politeness. Watching Charles's reaction as he'd studied the drawings, Robbie had seen true interest and admiration in those dark eyes.

Charles was the first person to care about his talent or mention that he had any. Of course, M. Richaud had found Robbie's work worthwhile, which counted for a great deal, but there was something even more satisfying about having someone close to him offer him praise.

"Let me put my drawing things away, and I'll meet you in the library at the chessboard," Robbie said. "I'll send Stewart to move you there."

"For now. But soon enough, I'll be ambulating on my own with the crutches. Look."

Charles reached out to take hold of the arm of the chair Robbie had been sitting in. After placing both feet firmly on the floor, he heaved himself out of the chair and upright with a grunt. His forehead glistened with sweat and he swayed, but he remained that way for a full minute.

It was the first time Robbie had seen Charles standing, and it sent a powerful twinge through him—happiness that his friend had regained his feet, a thrill of attraction at how handsome Charles looked standing his full height, and dismay and melancholy as he realized their time together was limited.

Charles was absolutely right. Before that time ended, they would, they *must* come together again. Robbie couldn't go out into the world regretting the moments he hadn't seized, the opportunities he'd lost due to straitlaced foolishness.

"Well done, Charles," he said. "I'm so proud of how far you've come in such a short time."

The smile Charles gave him as he dropped back into his chair wasn't smug at all. In fact, to Robbie, it appeared shy, touched by the compliment. More of the angel than the devil about this diffident Charles.

Impulse grabbed him, and Robbie stepped over to the man in the wheelchair. He brushed his hand through that lovely ginger hair and let it rest on the warmth of Charles's head for a moment, then he bent and pressed a kiss to Charles's forehead, another to his mouth.

His heart pounded as he moved quickly away, nearly rushing out the door with his sketchbook under his arm.

Chapter Eleven

The worst heat of the summer had passed, but the days seemed too sultry to Robbie. With the approaching dance, he had additional duties. He had an uneasy truce with Samuel, who seemed distracted and barely heeded him but at least didn't sneer or pick fights.

He'd just finished consulting with Aunt Lenore about the autumn-themed décor for the ball when he came across Gemma outdoors, sitting on the ground in the garden, clutching the squirming, nearly grown pup that she'd been allowed to keep from the litter.

"See, Miss Daisy? Wearing a dress isn't so bad. You just have to get used to it," Gemma counseled the whimpering dog in her arms.

"Gemma. Take that dolly frock off the puppy," Robbie ordered. "It's unkind to force her to do something that isn't natural for a dog."

"But she's so darling. Look!" Gemma thrust the pup, growing quite husky now, toward him.

"Perhaps, but she's also miserable. Take it off."

"All right," Gemma grumbled but obeyed, pulling one puffed sleeve down Daisy's foreleg.

When it appeared she was going to wrench the poor dog's leg, Robbie set aside his walking cane and eased himself down to the ground to help. The grass was still damp from another recent rain, and wetness seeped through his trousers and drawers. Ah well, they would dry.

As he undressed the struggling dog, Robbie wondered who would help Gemma with this sort of task when he was gone. Mary, he supposed, but the nursemaid wouldn't be so accommodating of her charge's lively nature, and soon enough, Gemma would be too old for a nurse, leaving only the governess, Miss Peters, to supervise her. Heaven knew Aunt Lenore scarcely paid the child any heed.

Robbie pulled off the taffeta skirt, then cuddled and petted the dog. His thoughts drifted, as they did every second or so, toward Charles, the other person he would greatly miss when he left home. With every day, Charles grew stronger. He could now walk with crutches. He was healing too fast, and yet Robbie couldn't regret that or wish him back into that awful wheelchair.

"Look, here comes Cousin Charles!" Gemma jumped to her feet and skipped along the flagstone path toward the man who strode determinedly toward them, one step, then a swing of the crutches. Charles planted the tips firmly before taking another step over the unevenly set stones.

Gemma danced around him. "You're doing well. But your face is all red. Is it hard to use crutches? I want a pair too. I want to play soldier home from the war."

Robbie's heart snagged in his throat and stopped beating for a moment as he gazed at the man who'd become far more to him than a mere friend. Sunlight set Charles's coppery hair ablaze. His shoulders and arm muscles flexed as they plied the crutches. True, Robbie couldn't *see* them flex under Charles's coat, but he knew what those arms looked like bare. He could imagine the subtle play of muscles under a smooth sheath of skin, and it sent a shiver of lust flickering through him. Good Christ, he wished he could admire more of Charles's body at great length and study every detail.

115

But time and privacy were hard to come by. Stolen moments were rare in a crowded household with family members and servants swarming about.

Robbie let the pup loose, grabbed his cane and hoisted himself to his feet. By the time he was upright, Gemma and Charles had reached him.

"...went off *again* without me. After he *promised!*" Gemma recited her tale of woe about negligent Bert. "He and Liam built a fort in the woods. That's all he'll talk about, but he won't take me to see it. It's not *fair!*"

"No. Indeed it is not," Charles said gravely. "Your brother should be horsewhipped for treating a lady so. Do you want me to do it?"

Gemma stopped and stared. "Really? A whipping? Would you?" She sounded far too eager and thrilled at the prospect.

"No. But I will talk to Bertie for you, if you like. Perhaps he'll listen to me." Charles dropped down on a garden bench with a grunt and set the crutches aside. The dog sniffed around his shoes, then squatted and pissed. "Is that the ever so charming Daisy?"

"None other." Robbie smiled. And smiled and smiled. He couldn't seem to stop smiling when he talked to Charles, or when he glimpsed him across a room, or when he even thought about him. All this smiling was going to get him into trouble.

The dog leaped against Charles's leg, and he leaned to take her onto his lap. Gemma leaned against him and prattled on about dogs and Bertie and the dress she was going to wear the night of the harvest dance.

"Will you save a waltz for me?" Charles asked.

"That's silly. You can't dance. Besides, I shall only be presented, then sent back up to the nursery. But Mary said she and I can watch the company arrive through the railing above the staircase, and she said I'd have a special treat to make up for not being allowed to see the dancing. Mary's nice sometimes." Gemma sighed and let Daisy lick her hand. "It's hard to be small. I can't wait to grow up."

Robbie ached at her forlorn tone. He came over and rested a hand on her head. "Don't be in too much of a hurry, sweetheart. Enjoy your dolls and dogs and fairy tales while you may."

Charles tipped his head back to look up at Robbie, and patted the bench beside him. "Sit. You'll put a crimp in my neck looming over me like that."

Robbie happily sat on the small bench, hip to hip with Charles. It was the first contact they'd managed today.

Some days it was easier to steal a kiss or a touch than others. Robbie was still working with Charles to strengthen his leg, which provided many hours spent close together in privacy. They could talk then, but little more than that. Since the first time Samuel had burst into the library, the room no longer felt so safe and private. Robbie's fear of discovery was too great and he would not so dishonor his uncle as to seize passion beneath his very roof. Now, if they could but take a ride out into the countryside or a ramble in the woods... But for now, sitting side by side on a garden bench in the warm sunshine would do.

In a bit, Gemma left to take Daisy back to the kennel, leaving the two men alone at last. The moment she was out of sight, Charles reached for Robbie's hand. Robbie nearly gasped at the warm strong palm pressed against his, at their fingers linking together. The sedate touch prompted nearly as much excitement as their kisses had on that amazing night coming back from the village.

How many times had he relived that event in the days since? The sensations seemed etched in him permanently; the rough wool of Charles's trousers under his hand, the silk of his skin, a hard mouth demanding things Robbie's mouth had never given before, the scrape of chin stubble against his own

117

chin, the wetness of a tongue swirling around his. Oh, and that was only the beginning. If he started to dwell on the other part, he would be lost in the memory for minutes at a time, jerking out of his trance with a start only when Mr. Todd asked him a question.

Right now his cock began to stir from the mere touch of Charles's hand and the memory of how that hand had felt touching him.

"Why, my good man. I fear you are having unwholesome desires. I can see it in your eyes," Charles murmured. "Bad, bad Robbit. How I'd like to take you someplace much more private and give you the spanking you richly deserve."

Robbie startled and nearly pulled away his hand. A jolt of dismay and incredible desire shot through him. His erection grew instantly stiff and aching and pressed against his trousers. He shifted on the hard bench.

"You like that sort of talk, eh?" Charles continued to whisper in a hoarse yet velvety voice that stroked Robbie's skin and made it crackle with electricity. "You like the idea of being bent over a desk and receiving a paddling on your rear?"

"What are you doing?" Robbie whispered even more quietly although there was no one nearby. "What outlandish things to say!"

"Too soon? Yes, since we've hardly done more than kiss and fondle one another. Perhaps you would not enjoy that sort of play," Charles said. "But it's fun to think about, isn't it?"

"I don't understand."

Charles smiled and stroked the back of Robbie's hand with one idle thumb, the little circles sending shockwaves of desire through him. "No, of course not. I forget sometimes how innocent you are. But that's fine. I shall be content with an occasional kiss for now. And perhaps, someday very soon, we can find a way to spend an entire afternoon together in absolute privacy. Then I can teach you more about how to give and receive pleasure."

Yes, please. He would be an eager student. The very idea of giving and receiving pleasure, whatever that entailed, made his entire body tighten. He wanted to feel, to experience, to *know* what all he might do with Charles. His rear tingled and his arsehole clenched in response to the thought.

"But that day isn't today." Charles released his hand, and Robbie nearly whimpered in disappointment. "Right now, sir, I should like to talk to you about your wardrobe."

"My wardrobe?" Robbie repeated dumbly.

"Yes. For all that you're a student of design and enjoy beautifully appointed rooms, you do not seem to turn that artistic eye on your personal appearance. I should like to help you outfit yourself for your new life in London—"

"Or Durham."

"Your new life in London," he repeated firmly, "And for the upcoming harvest ball. A man as fine looking as you should not hide his attributes under dowdy attire."

"You think I'm fine looking? Wait. You think my clothes are dowdy?"

"They are. It's not an opinion. It's a fact. With Cousin Phillip's permission, I have contacted a tailor from the city to fit you for several articles of clothing, including eveningwear. He has just arrived and is setting up as we speak."

"I couldn't possibly afford... When did you arrange all this?"

"It's quite all right. Phillip agreed with me that he owes you a decent wardrobe. Besides, Samuel wants a new suit, and Phillip needs one as well. I understand hosting this harvest event is an important thing around here. Even Phillip wishes to make a good impression."

Charles leaned to pick up the crutches and dragged himself upright. "So, if you'll accompany me inside, I will show you the wonders of *haute couture.*"

The next hour or so was a bewildering barrage of fabric swatches and decisions about cut and style. The tailor treated Robbie like a mannequin, measuring every part of him and holding material near his eyes to choose the perfect hue. Charles approved or disapproved each option while Robbie merely shrugged when asked his opinion. He didn't like being the focus of attention and was eager for the ordeal to end. After the last measurement, the tailor set him free and asked them to summon Samuel to be fitted for a new suit.

As they walked down the hall, Charles regarded Robbie with twinkling eyes. "Wasn't that fun? Nothing like being fitted for new clothes. You shall cut a swath at the ball. Heads will turn."

"It will only be me dressed in a new suit. I hardly imagine anyone will suddenly view me differently."

"You underestimate the power of style. They say *the suit makes the man,* and while that may not be true, it certainly colors how people view him." Charles thumped into the larger of the family's two drawing rooms with Robbie behind him, and dropped onto one of the sofas with a relieved sigh.

"You shouldn't overdo," Robbie warned as he sat in an armchair facing Charles. "You've only just regained your legs, and you should not push yourself too hard. Perhaps it's time for an afternoon rest."

"Yes, Doctor. I shall do that as soon as my bedchamber is not being used as a fitting room."

It had made the most sense for the tailor to unpack his supplies downstairs, where Charles could have access, but now he was banished from the library until the tailor had finished with Samuel and Phillip.

"Anyway," Charles went on, "it's not merely a matter of new clothing. It's the confidence a well-chosen wardrobe instills in you which makes you stand a little straighter, appear a little bolder."

"I doubt I shall ever stand much straighter," Robbie said dryly. "And my nature is not bold. I'm afraid I'm simply an accommodating sort of person."

"Which I adore. Your nurturing spirit is what makes you Robbie. Still, there are times when one must assert oneself. Trust me, when you head into the social waters of the city, you do *not* want to appear timid. Those sharks will devour you."

Robbie frowned, not wanting to think too much about the future. "I shan't be spending much time in society, I don't think."

Now Charles frowned, too, and leaned toward him. He seized Robbie in his intense gaze. "Listen. What exactly is it you hope to do when you leave here? Do you have a plan?"

"Well, uh, Uncle Phillip has some acquaintances who might find a position for me, perhaps working in accounts..." Robbie trailed off.

"What do you *want* to do, Robbie? I can't imagine you being content working in some stodgy offices for the rest of your life. I remember what you said about your time with that designer in London. You must try again. You are an artist at heart. If décor is what inspires you, then you must hobnob in society, making connections with the people for whom you wish to design."

The force of Charles's conviction was both thrilling and annoying. His words made Robbie see a vision of one possible future laid out before him, golden and fulfilling. But having a vision and making it happen were two very different things. Easy for Charles to tell Robbie what to do with his life when the man hadn't figured out his own yet.

"I suppose," he answered noncommittally since he didn't wish to argue.

"The way you present yourself is important. When you design a space, you present a particular view of the people who will inhabit that room, the manner in which they might wish to be seen by their peers. Choosing clothing is no different. You attire your body in the way you hope to be viewed, as confident, self-assured, in charge. Whether this reflects the way you really feel inside doesn't matter."

Robbie smiled and picked at a bit of stuffing peeking through a worn spot in the arm of the chair. "Apparently you've given this a lot of thought."

Charles sat back, resting his arms along the back of the couch. "I have. I think about you going off into the world, and I want only the best for you. I want *success* for you. My comments on your appearance don't reflect at all on how I personally view you. I adore your outdated clothes and your rather ill-cut hair. They are absolutely endearing to me, my Robbit. And, to quote Samuel, *Lord*, that sounded patronizing!"

"A bit." Yet he didn't mind. Charles's affection for him touched him, and he'd come to love that silly nickname. "Anyway, I do see your point. So it will be best foot forward for me at this dance." He tapped his lame foot. "A chance to practice hobnobbing."

Dread flickered in him at the thought. He'd become far too accustomed to being around only family members and servants, safe in this little nest called home. Now he must stretch his metaphorical wings and rehearse for the day when he would venture into open skies, leaving family and safety...and Charles Worthington behind.

That last was impossible to imagine doing without. Robbie glanced at the closed door, then leaned forward and rested a hand on Charles's knee, kneading lightly. Charles's eyes lit up, and his lips parted.

"We must take another carriage ride," Robbie whispered.

"Agreed. Why, I do believe we need to go into the village so you may visit the barber. Do something about that shaggy mop, eh?"

"Yes. Why not tomorrow?" Reluctantly Robbie took his hand away from Charles's warm knee beneath the soft wool. He slapped his palms on his own legs, set his cane and stood. "But now, I must get on with my day. Mr. Todd wants to review some accounts with me."

"Tomorrow, then." Charles's deep, husky voice made the words a promise that sent squirrels running up and down Robbie's spine. "And later today too, if you want to help me with my leg exercises."

"That would be my pleasure."

Robbie walked out of the room, smiling, smiling, smiling and whistling a little as he headed toward Uncle Phillip's office.

Chapter Twelve

Charles knew that Robbie didn't often allow his desire to surface and he even more rarely admitted its existence. Robbie actually stated that he wanted to go out in the carriage with Charles—and wasn't that a delicious idea. Perhaps the conversation about the future had added some boldness to his usual nature.

Or perhaps he was thinking of a time when he would be gone from the hall and unable to touch Charles again.

Charles had managed to neatly avoid those thoughts, and he even managed to avoid all conversations with Phillip. The future, so bright for his Robbie, still loomed gray for himself. But it was a brighter gray, perhaps a rainy morning and not a late-Sunday-in-November shade now that his health improved.

He pushed to make himself better, but he still flagged quickly. Charles felt exhausted from his morning's exertions, and what had he done? Walked in the garden, sat and supervised Robbie's fitting, then walked to the parlor and sat some more. Damn, his lack of energy was frustrating. He wanted to be able to jump up and run, simply flat-out run like a horse given its head. But for now, freedom was still not in his grasp. He should be grateful even to be on crutches. It was a huge step forward for him—pun intended.

Charles stretched out on the sofa, not quite full length as it was too short. He rested his head on a lace-and-bead-covered pillow and slung an arm over his eyes. This wasn't the most comfortable spot for a cat nap, but it would do.

He pulled out his mental list of professions, trying to decide which he could undertake—his usual method to while away time when alone. A small creak brought him from a half doze to full alertness.

He almost called out a warning so whoever entered the room wouldn't be surprised by his presence, but a quality to the soft footsteps made him curious. Someone was making an effort to sneak, and if he spoke, they'd either flee or stop pretending stealth.

Charles feigned sleep and through nearly closed eyes, watched Samuel walk quietly about the room. He carried a small leather satchel, the type a doctor might employ, folded open. Samuel walked to an occasional table, picked up a silver vase and unceremoniously dumped it into the bag.

God above, the boy was stealing from his own family. Charles wondered if he should speak up. But no. This was none of his affair, after all.

What would Robbie say if Charles employed that argument with him? He'd point out that one of the footmen or the maids would get the blame should the items go missing. That was unacceptable. Anyone in any position of power must do what he could to prevent suffering in the lower classes. Charles stifled a sigh. He was hardly in a position of power, he argued with the imaginary Robbie.

That Robbie spoke with his mild, calm voice. *Noblesse oblige was the proper attitude even for those without a drop of noble blood. You have several drops in your blood, Worthington, and an ocean in your upbringing—that education and rearing you've ignored for years.*

And you are a nuisance, he told the pretend version of Robbie. *I shall speak up when the items are discovered gone. Though I don't know why I would. I tell you, this is none of my business.*

But then the shuffling and soft clunks stopped. The infernal Samuel drew near. He stood almost looming over the sofa where Charles lay.

Charles opened his eyes and yawned.

"I didn't see you there," Samuel said.

"Obviously." The word slipped out filled with dry scorn. So much for the pretense that he knew nothing. He looked at the leather satchel and raised his eyebrows. "Allow me to guess. You need money, and your father refuses to advance you any."

Samuel turned white, then his cheeks flooded with red. "It's none of your business."

And what a pity this idiot would echo his inner voice. Really, he should have guessed that Samuel would easily fill the role of his less admirable self.

Meaning the better part of himself was Robbie. He almost smiled at the thought.

"What will you do?" Samuel said in a low throbbing voice.

"I'll hope you put the things back."

"You will tell my father."

"Not at all. I have no interest in dramatics, but my distaste includes the fuss that arises when valuables are stolen."

Samuel sank into a chair near him. His hands trembled. "I am in such trouble."

This sounded exactly like that horrible time not so long ago when Charles had finally understood his comfortable existence had ended. He wanted to rant at the young fool that he had no notion what trouble meant. But the sheer misery in Samuel's eyes was real. And perhaps if Charles had learned economy in his early years, he would have been able to save money enough to last through his illness.

"How did it happen?"

Samuel mumbled, but Charles caught some of the words. "My friends... Card games..."

"Ah, gaming debts. I've had some experience with them. I was foolish enough to borrow money when my family fortune began to wane. It's not easy to be a wastrel. One finds oneself constantly on edge and nervous. An uncomfortable way to live. "

"Lord, there's no one here in this godforsaken village that would lend me money." Samuel leaned back in his chair. He'd quickly regained some of his affected petulance.

"You should be thankful for that. The only rates available to young fools are far too expensive. Better you should go to your father and admit the truth."

Samuel's eyes widened. He slumped again and looked as if he was about to be sick. "No," he whispered hoarsely. "Never."

"You might ask your cousin, then. Robbie might know how to help."

Samuel rolled his eyes. "Lord, that stick in the mud would have no notion of what to do. You'd advise me to ask Gemma next."

He got up and began to pace the room. He left the bag sitting on the floor near Charles's sofa. Charles sat up and drew the bag to him. The youth had snatched several pieces of delicate brass sculpture, several ivory pieces, a Staffordshire shepherdess, two silver vinaigrettes and an antique Chinese fan in a box. He'd been through other rooms of the house already and had a strange mix of expensive and nearly worthless items. The gilt-and-glass paperweights he'd grabbed were hardly worth more than a few bob.

"What shall I do?" Samuel moaned.

Charles looked up from his inventory of the satchel. "Don't you have a pair of horses?"

"Jupiter and Apollo, yes." Samuel stopped and put his hands on his hips.

"You can't sell items that don't belong to you. Those geldings are yours. Sell them."

"I can't! They were a gift from my father."

"Then explain to him why you need to sell them. Get an advance on your allowance or your inheritance if that's not enough. My advice to you is to come clean. Tell Phillip or tell Robbie. They'll find a good solution."

Samuel rolled his eyes. "You can't help, I suppose."

"Samuel, I barely own the clothes on my body. What's more, I am the worst sort of poor relation. I was once like you, a spendthrift and gambler. I'm not like the dear old auntie who knows how to make do with a crust of bread and a smear of jam for months at a time. You should take lessons from that sort of auntie before you turn into me." He stopped to consider. "Perhaps that is how I could make my way in the world. Hire myself out as an object lesson for any young fool."

Samuel gave an inarticulate snarl of frustration. "I don't know how you can be so frivolous when my life is falling apart."

Sudden fury rippled through Charles, and he couldn't hold back. "Your life, you overdramatic lump of excrescence, is hardly falling apart. You have a family who loves you, a roof over your head and your good health. You will solve none of your problems if you indulge in self-pity. It is time to come to terms with your debt. The solutions will be difficult, but they hardly mean your life is over. And even better, once you do face up to the responsibility and pay off your debt, you will be free to start again with no real lost opportunities. So stop feeling sorry for yourself and stop stealing from other people to solve problems you created. And while you're at it, stop treating your cousin so badly. He's worth a few dozen of you, you insolent, insufferable whelp, and you should treat him with respect."

"Charles? Is something wrong?"

Oh Christ. The voice coming from the hall was Robbie.

Samuel glared at Charles. "Don't you dare say a word to the saintly Robert," he hissed at Charles.

"No, of course not."

Samuel grabbed the satchel from Charles's lap and backed away, feverishly buckling it shut.

Robbie opened the door.

"Nothing is wrong," Charles said. He smiled. "Your cousin and I are having a disagreement. That's all."

Samuel looked at Robbie and then at Charles, who should never have smiled so fondly nor spoken of Robbie with such passion. What had Samuel witnessed in that moment?

Too much, apparently. "Oh my God. It is just as I thought. You two!" He shook his head. "I saw that sketch of him you did, Robbie. Shouldn't leave your notebook where people can glance through it."

Charles wondered if Samuel had snooped amongst Robbie's things as well, looking for something to sell or use for money. "It's no crime for an artist to draw his friend," he said.

Samuel glared at him. "I know that. There was a picture of Gemma and her pup in there too, so I convinced myself Robbie was using whatever models were at hand. Still, there was something... I could sense it, and now I see the way you *look* at each other."

"What are you talking about?" Robbie said. His voice wavered, which made him sound unconvincing.

"I have no proof. But, by God, if I did, I'd make sure Father knew exactly what you both are. I've met men and boys like you at university. But I can't believe in my own family!" Samuel continued, "Saint Robbie has feet of clay. Lord, I'm sick just thinking of—"

"If you do anything to hurt your cousin, I will destroy you," Charles said in a low voice. "Do you understand, Samuel? I may have no money and my influence in London isn't what it once was, but I have enough. I will destroy you utterly and forever."

"An abominable creature shouldn't be tossing around threats."

"A creature like me has nothing left to lose, you idiot."

Robbie still stood frozen on the threshold. "What are you talking about?"

"You know perfectly well what I'm talking about, you sodomite." Samuel clasped the bag of family treasures in his arms as if he was holding tight to a baby.

Robbie resembled his cousin now, his skin going white and then red splotches forming in his cheeks. But his silence damned him and damned Charles. But really, what could he do? Charles wondered glumly. Shout out a denial? Robbie wouldn't lie.

Samuel started for the door. Robbie held up a hand, palm out, to stop him. "I know you and I are not the friends we were as boys. But I hadn't thought you'd want to...to destroy me."

"As your very good friend Charles would point out, it is your own actions that would destroy you."

Bad time for the young louse to develop intelligence and articulation, Charles reflected.

"I've hurt no one," Robbie said. He lowered his hand and stepped aside.

Samuel shifted back on his heels. He again looked from Charles to Robbie. Back and forth as if trying to measure their combined threat just as he'd correctly measured their shared affection.

"If you keep your mouth shut" —Samuel spoke only to Charles— "then I'll do the same."

Charles studied Samuel. He'd never looked more like Robbie, pale, with strong emotion shining in those eyes, his mouth clamped tight with banked passion.

"What happens when someone notices?" Charles hoped Samuel understood his meaning. *When someone sees the items have been removed.*

Samuel's next words showed he understood. "Well. You want to be Cousin Robbie's knight, don't you? You might take the responsibility, then."

Take the blame and avoid Samuel's carrying tales. Blackmail, but a nice bit of mutual blackmail. So many considerations crowded Charles's mind at once. Did he want to help this fool steal from his own father? A far more important consideration was the mayhem Samuel might cause with his tales. Being accused as a thief wouldn't destroy Charles the way it would Robbie, who valued his uncle's good opinion.

If Charles took the responsibility for Samuel's thievery, would Phillip have him sent to prison? He doubted it. But what would he do if—when—Phillip tossed him out? His health had improved a great deal. Perhaps he could even return to London, look up some of those friends who'd avoided him during the worst of his illness.

They might feel guilty enough to offer him employment as...as...and then the picture went blank. They might offer him work as a secretary. Yes, he could manage that. He might even make a fine porter, standing in a heavy overcoat by the entrance to some building, anonymous—

"What are you talking about?" Robbie interrupted his spinning thoughts. "Responsibility for what? Samuel, you should know that Charles is not to be blamed for anyth—"

He must shut up Robbie before he confessed any sort of sins. Charles blurted, "Yes. All right, Samuel. We have a deal.

My silence for yours. And I will shoulder whatever comes from... Well. I think we should discuss details later."

The punishment he'd face would be bearable. After all, he wasn't an innocent man. *If I'm not guilty of that crime,* he thought as he watched Samuel march away without a backward glance, *I'm sure I'm guilty of something.* Too bad it wasn't more sodomy with Robbie.

Robbie came to the sofa, but not so close that they might touch. "Why are you smiling? This is awful," he said.

"Your cousin is a tick," Charles remarked.

"What has he done? What sort of bargain has he forced you into?" Robbie demanded. He might have been damped down with a horrified shame when he'd first entered the room, but now he'd regained his spirit. That was good.

"Do you know those young buck friends of his? One has been sent down from the university, and the others trailed along after him."

Robbie nodded. "I'm surprised they're still in the neighborhood. I suppose they're holding out for the ball."

"Apparently, your cousin owes them money. He found a way to pay them off, and he wants me to stay silent about his methods."

"What is he doing to pay them back?"

"I suppose I ought to stay silent about his debts," Charles said slowly. "Did I promise him that too?"

"Oh no. Charles, tell me. I understand that Samuel knows." He only turned a little pink. "He seems to know about you and me. Does he have some other threat he can hold over you?"

"It's more what I have over him." Charles shook his head. "Never mind him. I'm sorry you came in when you did."

"I heard you shouting. And you were, uh..." The edge of Robbie's mouth twitched, then turned down. "It had to do with me, somehow. Really, you're hardly in any position to defend me or to threaten him."

"Yes, I know." Charles no longer felt tired. He grabbed his crutches and levered himself up and off the sofa.

"Are you going to tell me the details, or should I go ask Samuel?"

"Robbit, you can be annoying. All right, take a close look around this room. It's less cluttered than it used to be, thanks to Samuel."

Robbie looked at Charles, not at the occasional tables or the piano or the mantel or any of the other spots where Samuel had helped himself to objet d'art.

"That sack he held," Robbie said. "That bag had some of Aunt Lenore's treasures in it. He plans to sell those objects to pay off bills? But where can he sell them? Who in the neighborhood would buy them?"

"Your foul cousin is a mystery to me."

"That nonsense about you being my knight. What does that mean?"

Charles didn't answer. After a few moments, Robbie groaned. "Oh, dash it all. You are supposed to take the blame, aren't you? Why? Why would you allow Samuel to get away with this? We must go tell Uncle Phillip."

Charles clamped a hand on Robbie's arm. "No. Stop. He'll remain silent for now. We should too. We shouldn't be rash, my friend."

Chapter Thirteen

Robbie felt trapped in a strange whirl. For a few minutes after Samuel's confrontation, shame made him want to run away and never show his face at the Hall again. And then he thought of Samuel's threats to Charles, and anger replaced the shame like hot water following a showerbath of cold. He could not stay still. He could not allow Samuel to ruin Charles's life and his own. He could not imagine his uncle's face when the truth was revealed, whether the truth was about his son's thievery or his nephew's perversity. Robbie would spare his uncle those discoveries, so he didn't speak, and that evening, he was miserably weighed down with doubts about his own silence.

Aunt Lenore, of all people, came to his rescue, or at least his temporary rescue, from dark thoughts. The next morning, she came into the library bustling and fretful as she had been for weeks. The nearer the date of the party loomed, the more bustling and active she became—and also the more efficient and happy.

"You are able to go upstairs, Charles, or so Stewart says. If that's true, we will settle you in a real bedroom, not large, but it's pleasantly situated overlooking the garden. It's the room next to Robbie's. We shall have so many guests presently, I'm only glad we can find some space for you, our more permanent guest."

"Perfect," he said.

Robbie's heart beat faster, and he realized he would lock his doors at night and perhaps hide the key from himself as well. He eyed the wide staircases rising from the ground floor. Charles would do better using the servant's stairwell, which was far more narrow. If he took a tumble there, it would be easier for Stewart to catch him.

"Is there anything we might help you with, Cousin Lenore?" Charles asked. "Above and beyond Robbie's duties as head decorator."

She beamed at him. She seemed to have forgotten all about Charles's dreadful arrival at their home. And she only occasionally made veiled remarks about the stress of caring for family dependents in his presence. Her behavior to Charles moved between extreme solicitude, and those sighing remarks— with ignoring his existence her usual mode. This was much the way she'd always behaved with Robbie, although she frequently approached him with quavering requests for his help.

Once upon a time, Robbie would have begged her pardon for being an extra burden but now he only smiled when she made remarks about the extra mouths to feed. Charles, once he'd offered up his blunt apology for his drunken arrival, never apologized again. He'd made peace with Lenore and even did small tasks for her now and again.

Now Aunt Lenore was in another rarer mood, gracious and friendly. Not for the first time, Robbie considered that if his aunt spent more time busy with interesting activity, perhaps she'd be happier.

"You did fine work writing out invitations, Charles. I cannot think of a single thing you can do, since you are not as yet truly hearty. But, Robbie, if you have the time, I wish you would go to Durham. You may take the carriage, since you would have to transfer on trains and that might prove difficult for you."

He was about to protest that he did not mind trains or transfers, when she babbled on, "But you must drive, so I suppose the two-seater would do better than the fusty old traveling coach."

"And why am I to make this journey?" he asked when she stopped to draw breath.

"I just discovered they have sent up the wrong bolts of cloth for the dining room you planned. You ordered the loveliest buttery chiffon, and she's sent something bright mustard and stiff as a board. I sent that back, you can be sure. But now we must find something to replace it and can't wait for a trip to London. I have the name of a reliable gentleman with a warehouse in Durham. You shall go there as fast as you might and find a suitable replacement. You know best what will be a good substitute. It will be nearly a three-hour drive, so you'd best go along as fast as you can so you might make it back here before dark." She eyed the paper she clutched in her hand, a tattered list Robbie had made. "And while you are there, you might check with the man who is to recover the chairs as well. I hope he might come early. Do plead with him."

Robbie pulled out his notebook and jotted down her instructions. He'd been about to protest that the wrong fabric might do if it was washed, softened and put out in the sun to bleach the color, but suddenly had an idea that a trip away from the hall might be just the distraction he needed. He would take the quiet drive as an opportunity to think of how to cope with Samuel and, of course, Charles. But a moment later, that plan went out the window.

"I shall go with him," Charles declared. "And stop him from making a cake of himself in Durham."

She laughed. "Our Robbie never gets into trouble. I hope you don't mind if you go without a coachman or groom. I can't think of what Forrester is doing instead." Her forehead wrinkled.

Robbie supplied, "He is to help the footmen and Mr. Lester wax and polish the floors."

"Yes, that's it. Of course he must hitch up the horses and so on, but really. No time for more. So much left to do!"

Charles answered, "Robbie and I will manage your errand. That is one less thing for you to worry over."

She wore a broad smile and waved a hand at Charles. "I am grateful, of course, but I do think you are glad to go. A treat for you both. Now I must go find Mrs. Jackson to discuss dinner. We must eat even these days before the ball."

A yap came from the hall.

Aunt Lenore's smile vanished. "Gemma must keep her dog outside. That animal doesn't belong in the house." She fled the room, calling to her daughter.

Robbie made a show of tucking away his notebook. He had trouble looking over at Charles. "I don't know why you volunteered to go on the carriage ride. It will be uncomfortable."

"I think you can guess," Charles said.

Robbie could, and his breath clogged his throat.

Charles touched his shoulder. "We'll grab another moment of freedom, Robbit. When was the last time you were allowed to do whatever you wish?"

He couldn't help smiling and parroted the words back. "I think you can guess."

Charles had more experience driving, and his upper body had grown strong during his time at the hall. He pushed his crutches into the area behind the driver's bench and hoisted himself up to the bench, slow and painful, but without help. "At least this one has a leather cushioned seat." He flashed an entirely wicked and suggestive smile at Robbie.

Robbie clambered up next to him and stowed his cane with the crutches. For the duration of the drive, they'd be ordinary men with no defective body parts.

Forrester let go of the near horse's harness and tipped Charles a salute before ambling back into the stable.

"What I'd truly enjoy is a journey on the continent with you," Charles said as he directed the horses down the long drive. "Although I think train and ship would be preferable to any of Phillip's carriages."

"Yes, and when you win a great sum at the Durham Racecourse, we'll be able to afford your plan."

Charles sighed. "Except, after listening to Samuel, I promised myself never to gamble again. I suppose we shall have to take our journey via shank's mare with crutches as accessories. What do you think?"

"I think you're better. Even when you complain, you sounded lighthearted."

"You mean no more quagmire of self-pity?"

Robbie laughed. "You never drowned in it."

"And it's easy to set aside altogether when I have such delightful companionship."

Robbie wanted to scoff and say something about flattery and honeyed words, but he liked the outrageous nonsense coming from Charles. So he only grinned and leaned back on the seat.

The day was breezy and overcast, yet though the sun didn't appear, neither did the rain. The grass seemed brighter than usual and the air sweeter, and Robbie silently repeated the word "freedom" to himself to explain it.

When he glanced at Charles, though, he knew the real reason.

"It's not really three hours to Durham. Aunt Lenore doesn't approve of any sort of speed," he said.

"Yes, I know. Although, as rough as these horrible country roads are, the woman is right to eschew speeding over them."

"I have more than a guinea. I have brought my wallet. When we arrive, I shall treat you to lunch."

"And I shall be pathetically grateful. Much as I enjoy the food at the hall, it'll be a genuine treat to eat elsewhere, even if our meal is a workingman's lunch of fried fish. My only question is shall we stop for a dalliance before or after we enter the city?"

Robbie tried to speak but only managed a gargling sound.

"Dalliance is a euphemism," Charles said. "I'm thinking it could include anything from a kiss to full act of buggery—as described by the law passed during the reign of Henry the Eighth."

"God almighty." Robbie shook his head. He sat up and put his hands on his knees. "I think I vote before we go into the city so that I don't have to listen to your obscene mouth any longer."

"Mm. If I remember correctly, and I know I do, you're the one who spoke with passion." He laughed then, probably because Robbie's hot face glowed red as coals.

They drove on, and then Charles announced that if Robbie really did have a few guineas, he had the perfect solution. A room.

Robbie had no notion it would be so simple. Two strangers passing through a city as large as Durham could simply go to an inn, request a room for the night and sign a register. Whether they stayed for a night or only a few hours was no one's business. It wasn't like a small town where everyone's actions, even a stranger's, were scrutinized and discussed.

The keeper, a slender man with impressive side-whiskers and a striped waistcoat under a dark frock coat, barely bothered to look into their faces. After asking if they were to visit the cathedral or the marketplace and not listening to either of their answers, he made some comical remarks about the fisticuffs they must have had to leave them both lame. Though, he showed no real interest about them, he was a friendly, garrulous sort.

He talked and talked as he led them up the thankfully short staircase to the room. He apologized he had no rooms on the ground floor. He assured them that his groom would be gentle with the horses. He pointed out the beauty of the staircase they ascended, that had been built during the reign of Elizabeth and hoped they appreciated the carved angels on the handrail. That topic shifted somehow to the price of coal, then to the negligent ladies next door who failed to keep their dog from digging and soiling his garden, to the delicious meal he could offer them for only a few coins more. He took a breath only after he pointed out about the fine appointments of the room and the view of the street, which remained noisy for hours after dark, but what did one expect.

At last he begged their pardon and rushed back down to the public rooms because he'd just recalled his lady needed him below to tap a new keg. They did good business here, but it should be quiet by nine, he promised them.

"He didn't notice we had no bags," Robbie said faintly. He walked to the window. "Such a big city. I'm not used to all the cobblestones and noise." He wondered if he might explode with the nerves that shivered up and down his back.

The room was small, plain and tidy, with faded rose wallpaper. A lithograph of the goddess Patience weeping over an urn decorated the wall between the beds.

He'd rarely been in a room with so little personality and the nearly anonymous feel of it calmed his nerves—until he noticed the beds. Two beds. Both tall, narrow and neatly covered with matching white counterpanes.

Robbie stared at the beds for a moment, then turned his attention to the street again. If his uncle knew what they were doing... But he wouldn't find out. He couldn't.

"You look weary or sad. Are you, Robbie?"

"I'm tired of my own thoughts," he admitted.

Charles collapsed on one bed with a groan and propped his crutches against the flocked wallpaper. He pulled his injured leg up. "Abandon thought and kiss me." He squinted at Robbie, and his grin slipped a little. "Oh damn, you are still in a fearful state about this."

Robbie waved a hand. "One is oversensitive. Your leg hurts, doesn't it?"

Charles nodded. "And I have just the solution."

He reached into his charcoal sack coat and pulled out the small white jar of ointment Robbie used to massage his limbs. Just the sight of that familiar jar in this strange room aroused Robbie.

Although, to be truthful, the squat jar often made his lascivious thoughts drift to images of Charles half-dressed.

"You brought that along." Robbie laughed at the man's audacity.

"Of course I did." Charles unlaced and removed the black brogan boots—better made and cared for than the standard workman's brogans. He removed his jacket and slung it onto a chair near the bed. The waistcoat. The braces. He unbuttoned his trousers, and Robbie watched the fascinating show.

"I'm in real pain," Charles said. He lay on his back wearing only his drawers and vest.

Robbie removed his own jacket and rolled up his sleeves. He could do this, and the hunger to touch Charles's skin roared to life as it always did. So many days he'd rubbed and thumbed the heated flesh, his heart beating so fast he was dizzy. He'd held himself back from leaning over and kissing the skin. All those times he'd been in a stupor of arousal as he felt the weight of Charles's limbs in his hands, against his body.

He rubbed the ointment between his palms, warming it as always. The faintly medicinal scent of the ointment couldn't cover the intriguing smell of Charles, sweat and man.

And then his hands smoothed along the uninjured leg. Up and over the strong muscles and up. And on the impossibly soft skin of Charles's inner thigh that his touch had lingered over in the past. His own leg tingled as if Charles touched him in return.

Charles groaned and closed his eyes. "You have amazing fingers."

Usually he wore a blanket across his body, in case a servant should enter the library/bedroom. Now only Charles's fine linens covered his torso and the skimpy clothing hid nothing. Robbie watched the erection stretch and grow even as his own kneading touch turned into a caress.

All those hours touching this body, longing for more. And now he could. At last the feast was open for him. Anything else—the strange room, the thought of his family—vanished. He could do whatever he wanted, and God, he wanted so much. He'd waste no more time on delicate, useless regrets. They didn't have enough time, and he wouldn't squander another second.

He wrenched off his waistcoat and grabbed his own shirt and pulled it off over his head. His hands trembled, and he cursed softly when he had trouble with his own thick shoes. For a moment, he paused.

No one ever saw him naked. The doctor who'd watched over him during the worst of his wasting disease had only examined his limbs. The rest of him, his too pale flesh and his weakened leg—what would Charles think?

No more. He was done with fear and worries.

"Good, you're going to join me here?" Charles said, sounding surprised and pleased. "It's a bit narrow, but there's room for us both. Thank you, Robbit."

A moment later, he added, "My God, you're lovely. Such a strong, clean body."

Robbie paused as he crawled onto the bed. Why would he use the word clean? That word brought too much with it. He'd always felt slightly befouled with the weakened limb. He managed to say, "Hardly strong."

"Powerful," Charles said and drew him down into his arms. He'd discarded his own vest and wore only the thin drawers. Their chests met, so much skin touching. Robbie forgot his limp, forgot everything but sensation, and his breath hissed out at the pleasurable jolt at their contact. This. Oh God above, this was all he needed. But then Charles held his head and nibbled at his mouth, and he woke from the tiny reverie.

Kisses! How could he have forgotten that pleasure? They hadn't been able to exchange more than a few hasty touches of lips for too long, but now they had leisure for real exploration.

He writhed, impatient to get the perfect angle for his mouth to taste. Under him, Charles shifted, and his hip scraped over Robbie's painfully aroused cock.

Oh, yes. More of *that* as soon as possible.

He reached between them and unbuttoned Charles's drawers. He pulled back to draw more air and to admire the dark red hair and darker red cock. That was what he needed.

He shifted, moving down Charles's long muscular torso, impatient with that new hunger. Robbie wanted it all. His skin and his mouth and his hands and his cock—every inch of his body required Charles.

His mouth won. He'd taste the delicious flavor of Charles, the crisp hair of his belly, the tender skin of his cock. Robbie licked his lips.

Chapter Fourteen

In the many hotels where he'd stayed over the years, Charles had reclined on silkier sheets, rested his head on plumper pillows, sunk into more feathery mattresses on wider beds and had more skillful lovers tend to his cock. But no experience he'd ever had could compare to this moment, this wonderful, astonishing, one-of-a-kind moment with Robbie crouched over him, encircling his cock in one fist. As much as Charles might like to tell himself it was long abstinence that made that touch feel especially good, he knew it wasn't true. Not just any touch from any man would do. This was his special friend *Robbit* tentatively touching his lips to the moist tip of Charles's cock, then opening his mouth and slowly engulfing his erection in warmth and wetness. Robbie's awkward eagerness made the act better than any Charles had ever received.

It struck him that both times they'd been intimate, it had been the less experienced Robbie who'd taken the lead. Robbie had lunged at Charles and kissed him that first time before taking both their cocks in his hand and rubbing. Now it was virginal Robbie who experimented with his mouth and hands, sucking and stroking Charles's erection with enthusiasm.

Charles gasped as teeth scraped the tender side of his shaft and his cockhead hit the back of Robbie's throat. This was bliss and felt so good it took all his concentration to stop from spending quickly. He squeezed his eyes shut, slowed his panting breath and gripped handfuls of the sheet beneath him. He squirmed and thrust his hips up, begging for more.

Robbie sucked hard and slid a hand up and down the base of his shaft. He reached lower and cupped Charles's sac, fondling the weight of it and sliding one finger along the groove behind, that dark, forbidden, and oh so sensitive path leading to Charles's clenching anus. *More. More.* He wanted Robbie to trace the aperture and delve inside, but Robbie was not that bold. His finger withdrew, returning to rub Charles's balls.

No matter. This was fine. Just this—Robbie's hot mouth swallowing him down and his hand gliding over slick skin. Charles could hardly wait to return the favor. Robbie had never in his life experienced the sensation of someone sucking his cock. He'd made that clear in their conversations. Charles wanted to be the one to give him that. In fact, he should be providing Robbie first pleasure, rather than lounging here and soaking up all the delight Robbie gave him. But it was too late to interrupt things now.

Charles felt the familiar stirring inside him, tension growing into something nearly painful, trembling and wanting—no, *longing* for fulfillment. He would not hold back any more. He would finish quickly, not at all difficult given the strength of the lust rolling through him, and *then* he would show Robbie a good time, the best time he could possibly give him. Sweet, innocent Robbie deserved it. He'd struggled so long and hard against his inclinations. Now it was up to Charles to show him the wonderful reasons for giving in.

Robbie sucked too deeply and made a small gagging sound. It was that soft little choke that pushed Charles over the edge. The throbbing ache low in his groin exploded upward, barreling through him like a runaway horse. He groaned and jerked, chest heaving. His eyes flickered open, and he looked down at the beautiful sight of Robbie between his legs, mouth stretched around him, swallowing. It was a sight he'd begun to think he would never witness. His fantasies had centered more on him doing this to Robbie rather than the other way around. He hadn't imagined the novice would take over with such assurance.

As his tremors subsided and Robbie released him, Charles reached down and ruffled the man's hair. "You continue to amaze me, Robbit. Just when I think I can predict your behavior, you show quite another side of your character."

Robbie said nothing, just smiled and laid Charles's flagging erection against his belly, leaving it with a little stroke.

"And now, let me return the favor." Charles moved from his spot on the narrow bed, grunting a bit as he sat. He patted the warm spot he'd vacated. "Come. Lie down. It would be lovely if we could push the two beds together into one large enough to accommodate us, but I don't believe we could move one of them, even working together."

"No," Robbie agreed, glancing at the heavy frame, but Charles could tell the inn's furniture was the last thing on his mind. Robbie settled onto the mattress, his head filling the groove Charles's head had left behind on the pillow. He licked his lips, a telltale sign of his nervousness. "Like this?"

"Yes. That's just right. Relax, my lad. One would think you were bracing yourself for a doctor's examination. This will be much pleasanter, I assure you."

Charles grinned and moved a bit farther down on the bed. Given the limitations of his healing legs, he could not kneel over Robbie. Instead, he sat with calves over the edge of the bed, body twisted to face Robbie. He slid a hand up one lightly haired bare leg from shin to shanks. The man shivered beneath his touch like a nervous horse, a little uneasy but ready to run.

For several moments, Charles stroked his leg lightly, moving a little closer to the heavy length of cock jutting from the curls of dark hair, but not yet touching it. He judged the growing excitement in Robbie's reactions, the quickened breathing, the dilation of his eyes, the whimper he couldn't quite suppress.

"Are you quite ready now?" Charles teased. "For I wouldn't want to rush you. I can do this all day." Again he rubbed his hand up the thigh covered with wiry hair, grazed Robbie's balls with one finger, then moved away again, leaving him wanting.

"No, you can't." Robbie's voice was harsh, lower and darker than its usual light tenor. "Because Aunt Lenore expects us back before nightfall with the fabric. We have a limited number of hours here."

"True. Lenore is a bore. How I wish we'd simply told her we needed to rest up at the other end of our journey. Then we could have spent the night." Feeling the constraints of time binding him, Charles abandoned his play—which, given an entire day alone together, he would have carried on indefinitely, or until he had Robbie literally begging for his touch.

Charles leaned over, and his hips gave a twinge. Even though his lower legs had been broken in the carriage accident, the weeks of being wheelchair-bound had done something to his hips as well. These days it seemed his body was a conglomeration of many little aches and pains. He ignored the twinge and focused on the task at hand. *In* his hand, to be precise. He took hold of Robbie's erection and simply held it, savoring the thickness and weight against his palm.

He slid his hand up and down while gazing at Robbie's face. His lips were parted, and a soft exhalation came from between them. His head moved on the pillow, chin tipping up and throat arching as Charles gripped and slowly drew his hand from the base to the tip of Robbie's cock. The sight of that exposed throat set his heart stammering. He wished he could be two places at once, up near Robbie's face, kissing and nuzzling his mouth and neck, and down here, doing the same to his cock. But since he couldn't be, Charles focused his all on

Robbie's erection. He bent down and licked once all the way up its length, then blew lightly over the dampened strip.

"You let me know what you like," he murmured. "What you want more of. Because, Robbit, I plan to give you everything you want and more."

What did he like? Robbie couldn't think of one thing Charles was doing that he *didn't* like. The mere touch of the other man's hands on his most private places was beyond anything he'd ever hoped to feel. He simply had no words for the pleasure he felt, and so he gave a guttural grunt.

Charles chuckled. "I'll take that as a 'yes'. You do want more of this."

The hand holding him so securely in its grip had released. Now Charles was licking him—his shaft, his balls, tongue-bathing him all over down there until Robbie feared he'd shudder apart and it would all be over in an instant.

Steady on, he warned himself and tried to control his breathing. He was reminded of how he'd learned to manage pain when the aches in his legs had been much more severe than they were these days. It was all in the breathing. He'd learned to distance himself from the little woes of his body. This amazing, powerful pleasure throbbing in him was no different. If he wanted his cockstand to last awhile and not spend like a schoolboy on allowance day, he must master his body and postpone the release.

Robbie sucked in a breath through his teeth as Charles burrowed his face farther between his legs, *sucking* his sac and—was that audible sniff the sound of Charles inhaling his scent? Good Lord! That clever tongue continued to lap over his flesh, driving him mad. Occasionally, Charles would nip, adding just a touch of pain to enhance the pleasure. This was beyond what Robbie had envisioned one man could do to another.

Rubbing or even sucking a cock had filled his fantasies, but he'd never imagined the hedonistic *pleasure* Charles took in the scent and feel of his body, all of his body, for now a finger was lightly circling his bunghole and then probing inside.

"Ah!" Robbie couldn't suppress an exclamation at the unexpected entry. His muscles clenched hard around the intrusive finger as if to reject it. Yet a hunger deep inside him unfurled even more and screamed *yes, yes, yes!* He wanted that entry. He wanted to know what something even larger, something like, say, a cock might feel pushing into that far too small entrance.

Charles came up for air, his mouth and chin glistening and his eyes twinkling. "Was that a 'yes' too? You like what I'm doing? Then tell me so."

"Yes," Robbie muttered. "I like what you're doing. More, please."

Charming Charles. How could one look at that handsome, laughing face and not feel a corresponding joy? Robbie was filled with bubbling effervescence as Charles laughed and then resumed his business. His mouth engulfed Robbie now, plunging all the way down his shaft. His throat must be impossibly full, but the man never gagged. Up and then down again, his entire head bobbed. Meanwhile, his finger kept occupied with Robbie's rear entrance. It tickled around the circumference before easing inside, deeper this time.

Robbie's body relaxed, allowing—no, welcoming the incursion. He raised his hips higher to make it easier for Charles to reach him. He closed his eyes now, giving over completely to the sensations engulfing his body, rising and falling on waves of pleasure. The thread of tension inside him drew tighter and tighter, and he found himself panting for air.

Charles moved faster, combining his sucking with the brisk rubbing of one hand on the lower part of Robbie's cock. At the same time, he managed to add a second finger along with the first, stretching and filling Robbie's channel. The man was a juggler, able to keep several plates spinning without dropping one. And, oh, it felt so wonderful, so *right* that Robbie could not imagine why people could possibly think this act was wrong.

Then he stopped thinking as all the plates crashed together in midair and showered down in glittering fragments. His body spasmed so powerfully that he felt he might explode. The remaining bits of his brain went careening off into some other space, and he nearly blacked out as he forgot to keep breathing.

"Shh, shh, shh." Charles suddenly let go of him, threw his body on top of Robbie's and clapped a hand over his mouth. "Shh! Not so loud or you'll have the landlord up here throwing us out, or worse."

Robbie wasn't aware he'd cried out at the moment of release. It must have been quite a bellow. Now he laughed uncontrollably into Charles's palm, which smelled like Robbie's own flesh, a musky scent that wasn't at all unpleasant.

Charles chuckled too. "You're mad! Take hold of yourself, man." But the sparkle in his eyes belied his words, and Robbie could tell he was delighted by his abrupt loss of composure.

"You enjoyed yourself, then?" Charles teased. "Just a wee bit, perhaps?"

Robbie kissed the palm that covered his mouth, and when Charles removed it, he murmured, "You are a vain man. You enjoy hearing how good you are, don't you?"

"Don't need to hear it. I *know* it," Charles retorted smugly.

He rolled off Robbie, leaving his body barren and cold, and lurched toward the washstand to clean up. He returned with a glass of water for Robbie, filled from the pitcher.

Robbie accepted and drank it gratefully before handing back the empty glass. He looked up at Charles. "Thank you." He meant for far more than the water.

The man caressed his cheek, grazing it lightly with the backs of his knuckles. "You're very welcome. Thank *you*. And now that the cordialities are accomplished, let us lie here for a time and recover our strength before going to see about the fabric and the upholsterer."

Robbie could not argue, not when Charles was already wedging himself into the narrow bed beside him and throwing an arm and leg over Robbie to keep himself anchored in place. The weight of those limbs enfolding him felt too good. Charles's head nestled on the pillow beside his, a puff of breath tickling Robbie's shoulder with each exhalation. Oh, what joy this simple pleasure brought—to lie in bed with his lover, side by side, curved around each other, perfectly relaxed, perfectly harmonized.

"All right, then," Robbie murmured. "But not for long or we shan't be able to accomplish our errands and return home before dark."

That was his last thought before losing consciousness. That and *if I could sleep this way every night of my life, I should never want for another thing.*

Chapter Fifteen

Robbie woke with a start, blinking in the dimness, trying to focus on his strange surroundings. It took him all of two seconds to remember that he was in an inn, sleeping with Charles in a rented bed, and that it was almost dark outside. He'd slept more soundly than he could remember doing in a long time—certainly since Charles Worthington had arrived in his life. Since that time, his sleep had often been restless and filled with hungry sorts of dreams. Now that his hungers had reached fruition, apparently his consciousness had let go and dived deep into restful sleep.

Robbie sat up. Charles's arm slid lifelessly off him, but the man didn't wake. In fact, he snored with a soft rattle.

Robbie shook his shoulder. "Charles, wake up. We've overslept. Wake up!"

Charles opened bleary eyes and squinted at him. "What?"

"I said, we've overslept. It's almost evening, and we haven't accomplished any of our errands. The stores will be closing soon, and even if we left this very moment, we couldn't make it back to the hall before dark. Besides, we can't return without the cloth. What will Aunt Lenore say?"

Charles propped himself on one elbow, reached out and grabbed Robbie's flailing hand, which was trying to make a point about how serious the situation was. "Calm yourself. The cat's drunk the cream now. It's too late to do anything about it. We'll simply have to wait until morning, then return home. We'll say we had a problem with the axle or something."

"We can't *lie.* Forrester would know right away no work was done on the carriage. Besides, I'm no good at subterfuge."

"Then we'll tell as much of the truth as we can. We were unable to accomplish all our tasks. Darkness was falling, and we know how Aunt Lenore feels about traveling at night, it seemed better to take a hotel room and return home in the morning. She'll applaud our sensible choice when we finally do arrive, bolt of cloth in hand."

"You make it sound so easy. But right now, Lenore will be panicking. You know how she worries."

"Nice to have someone to worry about you, isn't it? Lenore may be as fractious as Gemma on occasion, but underneath, she is a caring woman." Charles stroked a hand down Robbie's chest, his abdomen, right to the soft place on his stomach, which he began to rub in small circles.

Equipped with a mind of its own, Robbie's cock started to rise. What did it care about aunts and obligations?

Charles stomach rumbled like a thunderstorm rolling in. "What say we go appease our appetites? Then we can return here and appease other appetites."

He patted Robbie's belly, then threw back the covers and got out of bed, leaving Robbie's cock twitching in abandoned bewilderment. He retrieved his crutches and stood up. His backside turned toward Robbie offered a sumptuous view of broad shoulders, rippling muscles and lean buttocks. Robbie took a moment to simply enjoy the sight as Charles moved around retrieving his clothing.

As he struggled to snag a stocking with the tip of one crutch and hoist it up to where he could reach it, Charles glanced over his shoulder. "A little help might be appreciated."

Robbie smiled and climbed off the bed.

In short order, they were dressed and outside of the inn, hobbling through less crowded streets now that the sun was down.

Robbie hadn't wanted to eat at the inn, so Charles had calmly approached a stranger, a traveling salesman reading a book next to the fireplace off the entrance to the taproom, and asked about other establishments.

And now Charles moved over the uneven cobblestones up the steep hill as if he lived in the city. He'd grown dexterous with his crutches, but more than that, he moved as if he belonged in this place. Robbie wondered if a country mouse such as himself could ever move so comfortably around city streets. During his brief time in London, he'd never truly gotten used to the clamor and confusion and the horrible smells.

"First things first," Charles declared and confidently led Robbie to the small shop that contained the GPO, the general post office. "We will send Aunt Lenore a telegraph."

"It might worry her when she sees the delivery boy at the door. I suspect she'll think it's a disaster. We don't get many telegraphs at the Hall."

"She ought to get used to it," Charles said. "The Chesters are well-to-do, and their world sends off telegraphs like most people use notepaper."

"You'd know, of course," Robbie murmured.

Charles filled out the form as if he sent telegraphs every day of the week. "We shall be vague." He read it to Robbie. "'Unavoidably detained, stop. Fine but must stay overnight, stop. Rob and C.'"

Robbie agreed. An Aunt Lenore scandalized by the expense would be better than one lying awake all night worried about the state of her relations and her carriage.

"We shan't be able to dine in style after this," he remarked as the postmistress took the form and his coins.

"We'll be fine," Charles said airily. Perhaps Charles was improvident and that was how he'd lost his fortune.

They next set off for the shop, also not far from the inn, thank goodness, since Robbie's legs were tired. They arrived just as the shopkeeper was putting up the closed sign. He allowed Robbie to come in and even smiled his welcome.

Robbie fingered the delicate yellow fabric. His aunt wanted a more unusual theme for her ball than simply the harvest, and he'd decided to create a dazzling display of sunshine and shadow, the two seasons of summer and winter meeting— skipping autumn altogether, or only showing it with a few orange silk leaves. He pulled the scrap of fabric from his waistcoat pocket. The dark blue Lenore had picked for the winter theme made the yellow gleam and seemed to almost glow. He stroked the yellow and made plans. He'd be sure to create some of the leaves from this fabric.

"Even I can see that's lovely." Charles peered over his shoulder. "Order buckets of that yellow, and Lenore will be pleased."

Robbie ordered a bolt, and the shopkeeper promised to have them delivered to the inn first thing in the morning. He also thought to ask the man to deliver a note to the upholsterer requesting him to go to the hall early. Good. The errands were completed.

"And now food, or we shall collapse on the street and be trampled by horses," Charles said and swung off in the direction of the restaurant.

Robbie drew pleasure from his confident boldness.

How much more pleasant moving to London—or wherever—would be if he had Charles by his side. An ally. A friend. A partner. During these past weeks of fretting about his future plans, Robbie had somehow never even considered that he might not have to leave Charles behind. Why couldn't they go off on this adventure together? Charles was nearly healed, much more mobile, and hadn't suffered another of those odd "fits" of tingles or weakness for a very long time.

Of course, there was the way Charles blithely spent money. Well. That would be something to discuss. Robbie knew husbands and wives argued about money. He smiled at the thought that he had already cast himself and Charles into those roles. Charles would soon need to find a job for himself and move away from the nest the Chesters had provided him. Why shouldn't Charles and Robbie move in the same direction? No one would question the relationship of two practically related bachelors lodging together in order to save funds.

The restaurant wasn't a grand establishment, and they settled at a plain wooden table with past patrons' initials carved into its top. Robbie was glad to see that Charles had no objection to cheap food.

Robbie, hungrier than usual, decided on steak-and-kidney pie. Charles ordered chops.

"I have been thinking about Phillip and Samuel and what we ought to say to Phillip. I think we should tell your uncle the truth—about his son, at any rate," Charles announced after the waiter placed the white platters piled high with food in front of them.

"I haven't been thinking about it at all today," Robbie admitted. "I suppose one shouldn't slough off an important matter, but last night it ran circles in my brain, and I grew tired of the topic. Today, with you, is such a holiday from life. I have not thought of the Chesters for hours."

Charles beamed at him. "I hadn't known you could be so carefree, Robbit."

He returned the smile. "It's a surprise to me as well. But so much of today has been." He ate some pie and reflected that even food tasted better than it had before. He even enjoyed the beer.

"Don't eat too much," Charles said. "I have plans for you later."

And just like that, Robbie lost his appetite—vanished because of a combination of apprehension and excitement. He set down his fork and knife. The thought of his possibly outraged uncle and thieving cousin hadn't put him off food. Pure anticipation did.

Plans.

Did he know what more they could do together? Of course he did. He'd felt Charles's fingers in his arse. Not such a leap of imagination there.

"It might hurt," he muttered.

Charles had just a mouthful of chop in his mouth, and after a moment's puzzled look, he suddenly began to laugh. After he managed to choke down the food and gulp some beer, he gasped. "You've been corrupted, Robbie. We will make it so you experience only pleasure. We will take our time."

Robbie didn't want to take his time. He wanted to go back to that inn and find out exactly what Charles had in mind. He wanted Charles naked and under him or over him or next to him—just so long as all that warm skin was his.

"You should eat some more. You have a lean and hungry look," Charles said, amusement in his voice.

"You're correct. I'm starved." Robbie pushed the plate away. "Let's go. Now."

Considering how badly their lower limbs functioned, they moved to the inn and up the Elizabethan stairs to their room quickly.

Charles sat on the bed. Robbie bolted the door, then went straight to the bed to attack him—or rather his clothes. "Hold still," Robbie commanded as he unbuttoned Charles's waistcoat. "I had weeks of practice disrobing you, and I plan to finally indulge in the fantasies I invented over those weeks."

Charles grabbed him and drew him into a kiss. Pulling back, he asked, "No longer awkward about what we're going to do together?"

Robbie smiled. "A little, perhaps. But you'll laugh at me, and everything will be fine."

The air had grown chilly, and the bedsheets were slightly damp, so they took a few minutes to warm each other under the covers.

"You're better than a hot brick," Robbie said as their bodies, gloriously naked, entwined and they pulled each other close.

Charles grunted, gave a little gasp.

"Your leg?" Robbie asked.

"What leg?" Charles wrapped him tight in his arms and Robbie could barely breathe, pressed against the firm heat of his torso and the thick, interesting bar of his erection gently moving against his own. Breathing was not as important as luxuriating in this perfect embrace, although at last he tunneled up so he could reach Charles's mouth.

They kissed, a slow gentle touch of the lips. Robbie pulled back to examine the so dear face, which smiled back at him.

They kissed again, and now impatience began to bloom, heat and longing and... Robbie lost the words for what that kiss and the feel of Charles, naked, did to him. He felt this new and impossibly huge need from his mouth to his fingers to his already aching cock.

He ran his hands over the long, lean body. Charles wasn't as thin as he'd been when they'd met—Robbie had memorized so much of him already. And now he got to gorge on the skin and sheer delightful bulk of Charles. He knew he could do anything, touch any part of Charles with any part of himself. Nothing they did would be wrong—it was impossible.

He wanted to tell Charles that fact; he understood that their caresses from a kiss to a pumping orgasm, was right and good, but the urge to talk passed when Charles reached between them and grabbed Robbie's cock, his grip firm and in control. He stroked Robbie once, twice, then licked his ear.

"If I don't get this soon, I'll go mad," he whispered. His breath chilled the damp he'd left. "Give me this." His other hand squeezed Robbie's arse, first one globe, then the other.

"Your leg," Robbie began.

Charles sat up. "Lie on your belly."

Robbie obeyed.

Charles's hand ran down his spine, and Robbie shivered, closed his eyes, waited. The anticipation for the next touch grew—but only chilly air brushed his skin.

"This damn bed is too small," Charles growled. "Move to the head."

Robbie opened his eyes and twisted to look at him. Charles's eyes glittered—and his body was magnificent.

Robbie crawled up the bed and rested his back against the overly elaborate bedstead

"Turn around, and perhaps you might hold on to that ugly thing. Yes, we will manage this nicely."

Robbie, naked and shivering, but not with cold, faced the wall and molded his hands over the headboard. Charles came up behind him, balancing carefully to keep the weight off his legs as best he could. He slid his hands over Robbie's sides, those long fingers exploring Robbie's chest, torso, a teasing, sliding touch over Robbie's granite-hard cock and his balls, already tight and aching.

Robbie pushed back, silently demanding more, and Charles plastered his front to Robbie's back. His cock, so large and so apparently eager, pushed against Robbie's arse. His erection seemed made of iron and the most enormous part of Charles's large body as it rubbed against Robbie's crack.

Robbie wanted to protest; he squeezed the headboard instead. Still Charles seemed in no hurry. He reached around Robbie and explored his nipples, which tingled with each passing tweak or brush. Charles must have put some ointment on his other hand, for when he grasped Robbie's cock again, the slip and pull seemed slick and easy, though so tight and...oh God. This was nerve-racking.

"Get on with it," Robbie said and pushed his arse back against the rod that moved up and down between his cheeks.

Charles huffed out a breath and pulled back. Now the only part of him that touched Robbie was his hand.

Robbie closed his eyes and concentrated on the feel of those slippery fingers, sliding, going inside him. He leaned down and rested his head next to his hands, crouched as if he was some kind of supplicant, and he was. *Please, please*, he chanted in his head. *Please let this be as good as everything else. Please let it start. Please.*

Those fingers were busy, prodding, pushing into him. And then came something enormous and slow, so huge he stopped moving and breathing to concentrate.

"Relax." Charles leaned over him again, that enveloping warmth against his back.

Robbie gave a short involuntary laugh. "I've never been less relaxed in my life," he said and then gasped as the enormous, implacable cock began its inexorable push in.

He felt invaded, and for a moment, in pain, but then he was conquered, and the pain gave way to almost too much pleasure filling him almost beyond capacity. And then, when that clever hand reached around and began to move on his cock, still better. Robbie swayed back a little to encourage Charles. That large body possessed him, and Charles could do whatever he wished.

"My body is yours," Robbie whispered against Charles's hand braced against the bed. Robbie wiggled. The pleasure might be too much, but he wanted even more.

Charles at last stopped moving forward and back so carefully and slowly. With a quiet curse, Charles moved faster, pounding into Robbie with his cock. And Robbie loved every single unforgiving push into his body.

He wasn't going to last. He strove to hold on, gritted his teeth against pleasure—waiting for what? Waiting for Charles. Together, he thought. He begged and threatened and pushed and reached behind so he could send them both over the edge. Charles slowed for a moment, and Robbie thought he might kill the man.

"Harder, harder," he growled. "Damn you."

Charles put a large hand over his mouth, and then he obeyed him. And he shifted just a little. Down a bit, so that the sensation grew sharp and almost painful again, and that would be too much.

"Charles, yes." Robbie sank his teeth into Charles's palm.

"You devil." Charles grunted in his ear. Three more deep hard pushes. So deep that the pleasure swirled through him, from his balls to the sweet pressure inside filled by Charles's cock that seemed to expand to fill every bit of Robbie.

The hand on his cock, the hand over his mouth, the body pumping into him—those touches controlled him now. He let go of the struggle. One stroke, two, and then orgasm seemed to explode from him, almost terrifying in its strength. He barely noticed the hand over his mouth tightening and convulsing in the same rhythm. Robbie gasped as the last of the tremors rolled through his body.

He panted hard, breathing through the fingers that still clamped around his face. As his heart and breathing calmed, he rubbed his mouth on Charles's palm.

Charles moved away, and Robbie sighed as he left. But his whole body still savored the struggle they'd been through together. He sagged against the bedstead and felt each stretched muscle and the stinging in his rear with a kind of happy triumph. Soon he would come back to himself, but for now—

Something wet brushed his back.

"Ah!" he exclaimed, then realized Charles was there, a flannel in his hand.

"I'm cleaning you," Charles explained. "Sorry the water isn't hot anymore."

Charles had limped to the washstand and come back with the cloth—and Robbie hadn't even noticed.

He wanted to take the cloth away and clean himself, but the circles Charles made with the damp cloth soothed him.

He arched his back and let Charles wipe his chest and stomach, where his ejaculate lay.

Charles had taken charge of his body as he'd ravaged Robbie. Now with his hesitant, soft touch, he cleaned Robbie's body and gave it back to him, better than before.

Robbie grinned at the silly thought. He slid under the covers and rolled onto his side. If they lay close, wrapped in each other's arms, they might both occupy the narrow bed. This might be the only time they had together. He was unwilling to spend any unnecessary moments away from Charles. Away, in this case, meant more than a few feet apart.

Chapter Sixteen

Charles lay in the dark, listening to Robbie mumble. The man spoke in his sleep, nonsense phrases, though Charles heard his own name once or twice.

When the mutters from Robbie turned into deep, even breaths, Charles shifted his attention to the still night sounds. A deluded rooster crowed far away. Nearer to the inn, a baby cried. A horse clopped by on the cobbled street. He'd grown used to the night sounds of the Hall—the wind in the eaves, owls and other animal cries in the wild outdoors.

His arm began to tingle, and for a moment, panic filled him. The strange symptoms starting again? But then he realized Robbie's weight on him had sent the limb into that uncomfortable state, so he carefully, slowly withdrew his arm.

He rubbed feeling back into it, recalling all those days and nights he'd tried so hard to do the same for his legs and his arms—without success.

It won't come back. The illness is over. Those were the words he'd used to himself through other long nights. Now, he actually believed the words. And even more astonishing, he wasn't even sure it was as important to his well-being as another silent chant he found himself repeating. Two words, repeated. *Robbie, my Robbie.*

The use of the possessive was funny because he'd never in his life wanted the work that came with the proprietorship of another person. He'd heard other men his age say "my wife" or "my child" with a kind of pride that he'd never understood.

Belonging to a club had been enough for him to feel he had people of his own.

He'd lost his immediate family, his parents, but those scars were old and familiar, the pain of their deaths turned into a whisper. He'd lost his money, and so his membership to the London clubs where he'd felt most at home. And soon after that, he'd lost his home.

All of those losses were vague unpleasantness compared to the thought of losing Robbie, or of never feeling anything like this uncomfortable, splendid night again.

He smiled into the darkness. He'd never been ambitious before, but then again, he'd never had to be. Since he'd lost his wealth, he'd gained humility and perspective. Now he must gain the right to call Robbie his own. Quietly, of course. He had no intention of sending himself or Rob to prison. The smile on his face grew wider. Speaking of noisy, they would have to live in a sturdy house, or perhaps out in the country. Robbie was not a quiet man when it came to pleasure.

The next morning, they set off back to the hall at a quick pace once the fabric had been delivered to the inn for them to carry back to the hall. The ball was only days away, and Lenore must be going mad without her chief consultant and dogsbody, Robbie, at her beck and call, Charles thought.

Gemma was probably looking for her favorite cousin.

No doubt Phillip checked his watch to see when he might discuss some estate detail with Robbie.

Bertie likely wanted to show Robbie his latest little sculptures. When Lenore had moaned about the boy getting underfoot, Robbie had given Bertie a knife and wood and carving lessons— providing a new single-minded focus for that young brain. Every few hours, Bertie emerged from the woods where he played pirate—usually in search of food and to track down Robbie to show him something or get his help sharpening the knife.

Samuel. Well. That whelp was probably imagining all sorts of horrible thoughts when he'd heard Robbie and Charles had been out all night together.

They'd nearly all miss Robbie, so vital to the hall, because Charles fully intended to rob them of their Robbie and make him his own. *My Robbie.*

If Lenore had been in a tizzy of preparation over the past few weeks, in those final days before the harvest social, the entire household was absolutely frenzied. There was barely a moment when Charles and Robbie could speak privately, let alone do anything more. No chance to run an errand to the village or take an excursion into the woods, and no opportunity to delve further into the topic of Samuel's stealing or his appropriation of their secret. Their overnight in Durham was hardly noted, such was Lenore's intense focus on the upcoming event. And, although Samuel's disgusted gaze lingered on Charles and Robbie, he kept his silence.

At last it was the night of the ball, and the whirlwind died to a dull roar.

Charles emerged from the small guest room on the second floor, which he now called home, straightening the length of his shirt cuffs so they protruded just a stylish inch from the cuffs of his dark tailcoat. He'd dispensed with the crutches and tonight relied on a tortoiseshell-headed cane that Stewart had dug up from the attic. Just as he took a step forward, barely leaning on the cane, Robbie's bedroom door opened and the man emerged.

Charles caught his breath.

There was little room for variation in men's evening wear. The peacock colors of women's gowns were denied them.

Gleaming white against stark black was a man's only option so far as color palette was concerned. Instead, it was the precise cut of a coat, the length of a sleeve, the drape of trousers—those minute details—which gave one's appearance a slightly different flare.

The tailor from the city had worked magic on Robbie's slight frame. The shoulders of his jacket were cut at a sharp angle and lightly padded to provide more breadth. His waistcoat emphasized his trim figure. And his trousers made his legs longer than ever. Like Charles, Robbie had a cane at hand, but this was not his regular crutch. The silver head of a lion peeped from between his fingers—a gift from Phillip, Charles knew.

Robbie caught sight of him and stopped. For a moment, they both stood, gazing at each other. The moment of silence was fraught with meaning, more than words could convey. Besides, in this busy house where servants darted about tending to guests from far away who would be spending the night, there was nothing they dared say aloud about their feelings.

"You appear very debonair, Mr. Grayson," Charles offered after a moment. "Quite the thing."

Robbie inclined his head. "As do you, Mr. Worthington. Are you quite ready to meet Misses Honoria and Celeste Brown?"

"Lead me to them. I shall be the most charming and excellent companion to ever squire a lady." Charles stepped forward, his limp noticeably diminished. "By the way, which am I to partner with, Miss Honoria or Miss Celeste?"

Robbie smiled. "It is quite awful of me, but I tend to forget which name goes with which sister, despite the fact that one is slender and the other rather plump. They have a tendency of completing each other's sentences, so one is never quite certain whom he is talking to."

"A hydra," Charles said. "Two heads on one body."

"More like the opposite. Two bodies and one mind," Robbie amended.

They walked companionably toward the stairs, Robbie telling the sisters' history in more detail so Charles would know something about them.

Charles caught sight of a shadow and nudged Robbie's arm. "Look there, a pair of ghosts haunting the festivities."

Gemma and her nurse, Mary, sat by the railing, watching the entrance of guests in the foyer below. People were arriving steadily now. The great double doors of the hall opened and closed over and over. Women with high-piled hair and feathered headdresses wore gowns of every rainbow hue and long gloves. Glittering jewels or beadwork caught the light, making the costumes glow. Their partners accented them like black velvet existing to show off the color and cut of a precious gem. No wonder both Gemma's and Mary's expressions were awestruck. The country gentry must appear like members of highest society to them.

For Charles, who'd attended much more lavish events, Lenore's party was less impressive. What held his attention were the expressions on the guests' faces. They were eager to be here, happy to see their neighbors, excited about this once-a-year social event. This sense of innocence, of countrified charm, touched Charles. He'd experienced far too much ennui among his set, who tended to observe life with bored indifference. It practically took an earthquake to stir them to any emotion. What a different world here, and how glad he was that he'd been forced to experience it. The mysterious illness and ensuing carriage accident may just have been the best things to ever happen to him.

Charles glanced at the handsome young man beside him, drew on his gloves, took hold of the banister and started down the stairs.

"And then I told Mr. Parsons that it simply wouldn't do." Celeste Brown spoke adamantly and too loudly. She underlined her thought with a gesture that set the many bracelets on her arm jingling. Charles was momentarily distracted by the flash of paste gems. He knew fakes from the real thing, and the Brown sisters did not wear real diamonds or emeralds.

"Simply wouldn't do at all." Honoria nodded so emphatically, her bejeweled headband slid to a new angle.

"I would have the entire order in full, or he would receive no more business from us," Celeste said.

"No more ever," Honoria agreed. "The gall of the man, trying to take advantage of two ladies."

"It's not the first time he's tried to cheat us on our meat delivery," Celeste continued. "These butchers. One must watch them with a gimlet eye."

"And one simply can't count on one's housekeeper to be aware of such discrepancies. That is why we had to let go our dear Mrs. Barney and now hire only a day maid."

"Naturally," Charles said smoothly. "Because you must run the household yourselves if it is to be done right. I admire your fortitude, ladies, and your economy. You make do under most trying circumstances."

He snuck a glance at Robbie, then wished he hadn't, for the man's expression nearly made him laugh. Not *at* the Brown sisters, who were actually quite sweet and pathetic in their faded gentility, but at Robbie's obvious attempt to bite back a yawn. The poor man's eyes were glazed. He looked the way Charles felt after spending several hours catering to Celeste and Honoria.

They'd met the ladies upon their arrival, brought them light refreshments and chatted with them prior to the supper while the rest of the party danced, then escorted them into the dining room and smiled fiercely throughout the plain and filling supper. Charles and Robbie murmured and exclaimed over the minutia which filled the women's conversation. Their world was very limited and their trials trivial yet oh so important to them.

Charles thought Robbie was quite heroic in his gallantry, so he strove to match his friend's single-minded focus on the sisters. It was easy enough to be charming and give the Browns an evening they'd never forget as they escorted the ladies back into the ballroom.

"Miss Honoria," Charles said when she stopped to draw breath.

"I'm Celeste."

"Oh yes, forgive me. I received a severe rap on the head during my carriage accident, and since then, I've had some trouble learning new names." Charles nodded at the gliding figures on the dance floor. "Would you care to dance?"

"Oh my." One gloved hand went to Celeste's ample bosom. "Are you able?"

"I do believe so, if we stay on the edge of the floor and move in small increments. Are you game, my dear?"

Celeste turned bright red at the scandalous endearment from a gentleman she barely knew. She fluttered a fan in front of her round face. "Why, I don't know... Usually my sister and I merely *observe* the dancing. I don't know if I should feel comfortable."

Charles extended a gloved hand. "Let us find out what we are capable of. Shall we?"

He took the lady's hand, tipping a wink at Robbie behind her back, and guided her onto the floor. Usually he loved to dance. He was light on his feet and quite skilled. Even with his lame legs, he was able to move in the familiar pattern of a slow waltz, one hand on Celeste's great waist, her fingertips resting on his shoulder and her other hand palm to palm with his. He could feel her tension. She was afraid of the contact and probably hadn't been this close to a man in years—or perhaps her entire life.

Charles guided her in the one-two-three glide of the dance. Small steps, a bit behind the beat and awkward, but they were moving. They were dancing. When the tension eased from Celeste's body, when her hand relaxed against his and her eyes started to glow with joy, her straight lips to curve in a smile, Charles felt like a hero, and he fully understood that a simple act of kindness perhaps did more for the giver than for the person being given to. How had he lived most of his life without knowing that?

As if he weren't feeling emotional enough, he glimpsed Robbie leading Honoria, a spindly stick of a woman, onto the floor. Robbie took her in an awkward embrace and together they shuffled around in a circle. Honoria's smile was as bright as her sister's, and when Robbie lost his balance slightly, she steadied him.

Charles couldn't manage an entire waltz. After a few moments, he guided his partner off the floor with an apology. Red-faced from exercise rather than embarrassment this time, Celeste waved off the apology.

"Thank you very much, Mr. Worthington. My sister and I have enjoyed this evening immensely."

Charles saw Celeste to a seat and dropped a bit heavily onto the one beside her, upholstered in exactly the perfect shade of gold, which brought back memories of his and Robbie's brief sojourn in Durham. What an amazing night that had been. How wonderful it would be to share a flat in London or Durham, or a small house in the country, or anyplace in the world where they could be alone together, away from prying eyes.

How would they manage it? With no money, it wouldn't be easy to launch themselves into the world. Charles knew Robbie had some savings, but as for himself...he was as poor as any beggar, beholden to the kindness of relatives. What in the world could he do to improve his circumstances? What skills did he have which might prove lucrative? He thought of the calligraphy he'd used on the invitations to tonight's soiree. Cousin Lenore had been impressed by his hand. Perhaps others might pay for such secretarial skills.

Lost in thought, Charles paid little heed to whatever Celeste was chattering about. He watched Robbie and Honoria move past, tottering a little but still on their feet. And then, across the room, he noticed Samuel leaving through the French doors into the garden. Charles frowned. Something about the furtive way Samuel had looked around the room before walking from it—no, skulking from it—set off an alarm inside Charles. The boy was up to no good. Again. He knew it at a primal level, but what could he do about it? Excuse himself from Celeste's company and go shambling after his young cousin? He'd never catch up.

And then Robbie and Honoria, breathless and pink-cheeked, joined them, and Charles stopped worrying about what Samuel might be up to. Perhaps the boy was simply sneaking off to nip a more potent drink than the punch provided at the party.

Charles smiled up at Robbie, whose forehead shone with perspiration. "Well done. See, I knew you could dance."

"Hardly. More of a shuffle really." But Robbie appeared pleased and happy.

Honoria sat beside her sister, and the two chattered and giggled like young girls rather than spinsters in their fifties. Robbie sat near Charles, and they spoke of this and that, including the success of the harvest ball and Robbie's dramatic color scheme. Lenore had given credit where credit was due, telling everyone that her nephew Robert was the architect of the event. Several people had come to him to compliment him on his artistry.

172

It was turning out to be an altogether pleasant night, Charles thought, rewarding in unexpected ways. But it seemed the moment a person began to feel too pleased with life, something must happen to tear down the thin veil between happiness and disaster, for no sooner had he thought this than Stewart approached them, weaving his way between the guests and heading straight for Robbie. He leaned down and whispered something in Robbie's ear.

Charles sat up straighter, the hairs on his neck rising.

Robbie nodded and rose with the aid of his cane. He gave a brief bow. "Misses Honoria...Celeste, please excuse me. My aunt needs my aid with something. I don't know if I shall be able to return before you leave, so I must bid you good-bye and place you in Charles's capable hands."

"Oh dear." Honoria frowned, clearly distressed at the idea of losing her evening's companion. "I do hope everything is all right. A kitchen disaster perhaps?"

"Something like that. Not to worry. It's nothing serious."

Robbie's expression said otherwise, though. He exchanged a quick glance with Charles before turning and heading off with Stewart.

Charles wanted to bolt up and go after them, but it appeared he was now the sole proprietor of the Brown sisters. Christ, what could he do to hurry them along home?

But it turned out he didn't have to offer the excuse he was inventing about his legs giving him pain—which wasn't actually a falsehood—for Celeste read the situation and noted his impatience.

"Well, Sister, I believe it is time we were off home. It has been a lovely evening in every way, Mr. Worthington, and we thank you and your cousin for entertaining us."

"Oh, must we?" Honoria cast a sad eye on the dancing couples still swaying and circling around the floor. "Could we not remain a little longer?"

"I think not. The hour is very late, and we do have Mr. Bracht coming early in the morning to assess the roof." She stood, effectively putting an end to any more protests from her more submissive sister.

Charles rose too and, despite his worsening limp, escorted the sisters to the door of their coach. He bowed over each gloved hand, one rather plump, the other as light as a twig, and bid each of the ladies good night.

As soon as the door closed behind them, he rushed as quickly as he was able toward the rear of the house. He wasn't quite certain where he would find Robbie but guessed it would be far from any place a guest might wander.

He didn't have to check many rooms before he heard raised voices, which led him directly to Phillip's office. Charles pushed open the door to observe a strained family tableau. Samuel stood before his father while Phillip, apoplectic with rage, jabbed the air in front of his face with one finger. Robbie had a hand on his uncle's arm, clearly trying to calm him down. Lenore hovered nearby, holding her head in both hands as if she could barely keep it from blowing apart. Tears streamed down her cheeks.

A further study showed Charles the painting had been taken down from the wall and leaned against a chair. He recognized it as one of the few valuable art pieces the Chesters possessed. A satchel sat on the floor beside it, a sable wrap spilling out from the open case. Immediately Charles understood. Samuel had been in the process of stealing from the guests as well as his family.

"How could you? What sort of person have you become? My own son, a thief!" Phillip thundered.

"Shh. Our guests might overhear." Lenore moved at last, approaching her husband and touching his other arm. "We must return these things before their owners realize they are missing, and then we must return to our guests before they are aware their *hosts* are missing!"

Suddenly all her flightiness had disappeared, and Lenore appeared a far sterner, more authoritative figure than the woman Charles had come to know.

"We will keep our family's reputation intact at all costs," she continued, staring first into Phillip's eyes and then her son's. "Later we will sort this out and come to some resolution."

She looked over at Charles, including him in her level gaze. "Mr. Worthington, will you kindly call in Stewart and ask him to aid my son in returning these items? You might also implore him to keep quiet about what he witnessed tonight. His position might depend on it." She cleared her throat. "And of course he should know we reward loyalty."

"Yes, ma'am. I'll make sure he understands."

Charles went to do her bidding. One had to admire a woman who knew how to apply the stick and the carrot so ably.

But his amusement was quickly subsumed by sympathy for Phillip and Lenore's agony at learning their son was a thief as well as a wastrel. He wondered if they knew the reason Samuel had felt compelled to steal. Had the idiot told them the extent of his gaming debts?

Beneath those whirling thoughts lay worry. He couldn't help but wonder what the discovery meant for him and Robbie. Now that their quid pro quo was over, what would stop Samuel from telling Phillip what he knew about their relationship? On the other hand, what would Samuel gain from telling? For Robbie's sake, Charles prayed he would simply keep mum.

But the nagging feeling that the night's dramatic events were only beginning wouldn't let Charles breathe properly. A small voice inside him warned that the brief time of respite from pain and problems was over. Trouble knocked at his door, and refusing to answer couldn't make it go away.

Chapter Seventeen

Robbie moved like an automaton through the ballroom, a smile fixed on his mouth and all the right pleasantries coming from his lips, but underneath, anxiety boiled. Why couldn't these people sense the tension and realize it was time to leave or retire to their rooms? They needed to end this event so the next act of the Chester family drama could play out. He'd avoided so much as thinking about Samuel for days, but now that the truth was coming out, he wanted it over and done. The violinist caught his eye and raised his gray eyebrows—one o'clock had arrived, and the musicians had been commissioned until that hour. Robbie signaled to the man to continue playing. The musicians must perform until he got word that the possessions had been restored.

Stupid, stupid Samuel. The boy may have been university educated, but he was an idiot. Did he think no one would notice their valuables missing when they got home? Did he not care that a servant would probably be blamed? Not to mention the Chesters' reputation would be permanently tarnished. Samuel gave no thought to anyone but himself. That had always been his trouble, even when they were boys. He took the largest piece, made sure he was first in any queue, and threw a tantrum when he lost a game.

Robbie's anger grew, and it was all he could do to keep smiling as he bid good night to the Holloways, an elderly couple who couldn't take their leave without talking for twenty minutes.

Now that he had a good head of steam built up, Robbie's ire began to spill over onto other people. Namely Charles. If he'd let Robbie go to Phillip when they first discovered Samuel's gambling debts, none of this might have happened. They could have helped the young fool find a solution that didn't involve petty crime.

But then Samuel would have told your secret, an inner voice reminded him.

Also Charles's fault. He wouldn't have *had* a secret if Charles hadn't pushed him toward the very thing he was trying to avoid.

Robbie knew that wasn't true. He'd taken an equal part in choosing to have a physical relationship with Charles, and he didn't regret it. Not really. Not at all, in fact. But right now he was angry, and it was hard to remember that he cared for Charles.

Jarrod Watersmith, one of the young men who'd dragged Samuel into this mess, and his visiting friends still danced and flirted. They hadn't a care in the world and looked fresh, though it was past one in the morning. And as long as those eligible bachelors remained, the few families with marriageable girls would hold out too. At least they weren't in the card room fleecing other idiots like Samuel.

The guests had begun to notice that the hosts of the event weren't present. One older gentleman, Colonel Fletcher, peppered Robbie with questions about their disappearance. That eager expression of interest on his thin face told Robbie that he wasn't going to take his leave until he knew the answer. If word got out, the neighborhood would dine out on it for weeks.

He must drag Aunt Lenore back to face the guests.

Stewart appeared at his elbow. "The items are restored, Master Robert."

He sagged in relief. With a few terse words, he gave Stewart a message to deliver to Aunt Lenore: she must show her face soon. The host and son could be absent—people would assume they'd stepped out or were taking their turn at the card tables in the drawing room. But when all of them vanished, talk grew sharp.

A few minutes later, Lenore reappeared. Her smile seemed tense, her back a little straighter and her face paler than usual, but otherwise she gave the impression of a calm, even welcoming, hostess.

She stopped to speak to Robbie, a smile plastered to her round, pleasant face as she murmured, "Did you know? Did Samuel tell you about his debts?"

"He does not confide in me, Aunt."

"No, and I wish to heaven he did." She stopped surveying the room to shoot a glance at Robbie, and for a moment, her smile seemed real. "I'm grateful to you for all of your help, dear boy. I'm selfishly glad to have you here with us. I don't say it often enough, I know."

The avid colonel spotted her then and beamed at them both. He began to make his way across the room, easier now that most of the dancers had retired for the night.

"Go to your uncle," she said quickly before the colonel reached them.

"Might I excuse the musicians now?" he said.

"Yes, yes, please. Then go to Phillip."

He wondered if his presence would help, but he was grateful to be able to escape the ballroom. With a bow to her and a good night to the colonel, he withdrew.

Charles sat on a chair just outside Phillip's office, his eyes closed. He started awake when Robbie called his name. Stifling a yawn, he stretched and pulled himself up slowly.

"Are you well?" Robbie asked, forgetting his annoyance at Charles. The man who'd been starched perfection at the start of the evening looked rumpled and a trifle dusty. His crumpled gloves lay on the floor next to the chair. Robbie leaned down and fetched them for Charles, who took them with a nod of thanks and drew them back on.

"Stewart and I scrambled about many of the unoccupied rooms—as much as I can scramble that is. Phillip had us search every inch of Samuel's room. We found more loot under the mattress and in the wardrobe. I delivered the odds and ends, including a packet of gambling vowels—that dolt is in trouble—and left father and son to sort that out."

"Why are you here?"

"Guarding the fortress while the attack occurs inside." He gestured at the chair, a sturdy wooden one from his uncle's study. "You sit for a while, Robbie. You look done in. You're not used to these late nights."

"Nor are you anymore." Robbie didn't argue but gratefully sank onto the chair.

Almost inaudible yet clearly angry voices came from the office while music and laughter floated down the corridor.

Charles jerked his head toward the office door. "It's the drama that wears a man down. I expect that Phillip will give Samuel the money he needs. I only hope that he'll make sure there are lasting consequences to the folly."

Robbie felt he had to protest. "He is a good father."

Charles leaned against the dark wood of the wall, shifting to fit his back between two carved panels. "Yes, and I would guess if he had a fault, it would be a tendency toward unyielding rather than too liberal. Now you, Robbie, would take the middle path between lax loving and hard-edged discipline."

"But I shall never be a father." In the past, he'd sometimes contemplated that fact with some sorrow. At the moment, hearing the muffled voices of Phillip and Samuel, he didn't feel the same measure of loss.

"You should have said something to Phillip," Robbie said, recalling his earlier surge of annoyance.

"You think so? But you didn't speak out either." Charles gave him a haughty look.

"I wasn't a true witness. It would have been hearsay on my part. You saw him take the objects, and you didn't speak up."

"No, I didn't. I am fond of Phillip. I'm grateful to him for giving me a home. But I am not bound up in this family. At least not with any member other than you. And don't forget that Samuel knows our—" But then he fell silent because the door to the office opened.

Phillip stood in the doorway and looked down at Robbie in the chair, and his brow wrinkled. "I thought you'd be— Oh, there you are, Charles." He twisted to peer up the corridor toward the stairs and the sound of the ball. He lowered his voice. "I need you to come in and tell me where you found these letters in Samuel's room. Robbie, you might come in as well. I have no interest in going over this nonsense with anyone else, and perhaps you might relate the details to Lenore."

Samuel stood in front of the desk, watching them, a dark scowl on his face. "Not him. Not Perfect Prefect Robbie. I don't want him carrying tales to Mother."

Phillip, moving to the seat behind his desk, didn't look up from the dingy scraps of papers he held in his hand. "I do not recall asking your opinion on the matter."

Charles gave Robbie a comical grimace and ambled into the room, leaning on his cane. Robbie followed and closed the door.

"You may sit," Phillip said.

Samuel went to a chair by the window, and Phillip barked, "Not you, sir. You will stand, and you will listen."

"But I say, Guv'nor—"

"And you will not address me by that absurd sobriquet. I am Father or Sir. Do you understand?"

Robbie was beginning to feel sorry for Samuel. He was not interested in watching his cousin's humiliation, so he levered himself up. "Perhaps I'll see if Aunt Lenore requires my help. The musicians will soon finish, but there are still a number of guests, and they might begin to wonder where we are."

Samuel's friends, for instance. Now that the music was ending, they might wander off looking for him.

Phillip finally looked at Samuel. "Now that is the sort of thoughtfulness I would hope a man would give to his family. Some awareness of the well-being of people other than himself. I've never seen Robbie act as anything other than considerate of other people."

Robbie closed his eyes for a long moment rather than face the burning fury he knew was on Samuel's face. Perhaps he could explain, tell his uncle that he was only trying to weasel his way out of the room. He had no desire to impress Phillip, just escape. Perhaps for once he might come right out and say the words...

"He's not such a blasted paragon, Father."

Charles cleared his throat loudly, interrupting Samuel. "You asked me where I found the items in Samuel's room. The papers were in the small desk in the corner of his bedroom along with the earrings, but I think I recognize the earrings as garnets belonging to Lenore, so we don't need to worry that a guest might be missing them."

Samuel snarled, "The earrings are Mother's. They're broken, and I promised to repair them." He pointed at the earrings on the desktop with a shaking finger. "See? The backing is cracked. I would repair them, dammit. Not everything I do is selfish. I'm not the worst person in this house, Father."

"Luckily, it is not a competition. But if it were, and if I were a betting man as you are, I'd put the money on you." The casual sneering unpleasantness was so unlike Phillip, Robbie wondered if his uncle had reached some sort of limit to his temper.

"The worst isn't me, it's your precious, precious Robbie." Samuel's voice came out in a cracked sob.

"Oh no, Samuel. Don't allow your jealousy of your cousin to make you ugly." Now Uncle Phillip only sounded bone weary.

The tears ran freely down Samuel's flushed cheeks. "He is! He is! He's in league with that other parasite."

"Samuel, stop," Charles said, his voice low and urgent. But Robbie knew there was no point. Once Samuel had reached that edge of anger, he couldn't be stopped.

Robbie's earliest memory in the family was of Aunt Lenore trying to soothe the wailing Samuel as he flailed through a tantrum.

If he hadn't been so afraid of what was about to come out of Samuel's mouth next, he would have been sorry for him, because he knew how much Samuel hated the loss of control he felt with those angry tears.

"You know what they are, Father! You just close your eyes to what they do because you love your pretend son too much. You love him more than you love me, your real son."

"Do not enact a scene, Samuel. You are a grown man, not a child."

"Yes, I'm an adult, so I know what sort of illegal filth is going on here. Under your roof and with my little brother and sister only a few rooms away." His crying convulsed him so much it was difficult to understand his words. Difficult but not impossible. He yanked something from his pocket.

"Proof." Samuel threw it on the desk. "You wrote about desire and Charles Worthington on the same page."

Oh Christ. Robbie had started a new notebook and entirely abandoned the old one in a drawer of his desk where Samuel worked as well. Shame and indignation warred in his belly. He'd been such a fool to write that vow, and a bigger one not to rip out the page and burn it. But what right had anyone to read his book? None. He must hold tight to the outrage.

Samuel had no right. Even his uncle had none.

"That's mine," Robbie said, managing to keep his voice calm.

"Let my father see what you wrote. He should read the filth you wrote."

"No." Robbie reached for it and tucked it into his pocket. "This book is mine."

Phillip had been reaching for the notebook, but now he shifted his gaze to Robbie, who stared back, unwilling to drop his eyes.

"The words are so awful you won't let me see it?" Phillip sounded amazed and hurt.

"The words are private, sir."

"Do you understand Samuel's accusation?" Phillip asked.

Robbie considered protesting ignorance, going through a long, stupid charade of feigning innocence. But then he recalled all he and Charles had done in that hotel room. He wasn't much of a liar. "Yes, I understand."

"Is Samuel right? Did you indulge in...in this criminal activity? Under my roof? God, if it wasn't bad enough that my son is a thief, you might be a sodom—"

"No. Not under your roof, Uncle Phillip."

"But elsewhere? And you *wrote* of it?" Phillip's cheeks burned as red as Samuel's. For the first time, Robbie completely understood his cousin wasn't the only one with that fierce temperament. Phillip simply had learned to control his version.

Robbie decided not to answer.

"Tell me, dammit. Have you...did you and...Worthington..." The words seemed to choke his throat. Philip slammed his hand down hard on the desk. "I took you and him in. I had pity on you...two..."

Charles was done listening to this. "Phillip, stop." He raised his voice to be heard over the sputtering anger. "Robbie is a good man, and that's enough."

"You! You're a corrupting drunkard."

Charles considered arguing, but the man had a point. He only shrugged instead.

Phillip rose to his feet. "And you dragged a fine young man into the filth and..."

Charles also got up, only more slowly. "Your son is yours to discipline and control. I am not your son." He couldn't help adding, "If we were to continue this conversation, which we shall not, I'd point out any actions I've taken have hurt no one."

"If these accusations are true, you hurt Robbie!" Phillip shouted now.

"Then the problem is between him and me." Charles pushed his cane against the floor and stood heavily. Damn, his leg and hip were painful. He did not have any desire to collapse in front of Phillip or Samuel.

Robbie was the only one still sitting. "I wasn't hurt, Uncle Phillip. I'm all right."

"Not if what Samuel says is true. Is it? Answer me, dammit."

Lie, Charles begged him silently. *Just smile and lie, and we'll leave without any more of this nonsensical drama. Let him*

185

read the damn book and tell him the desire you wrote about was only for Charles to witness, not be a part of.

Instead, Robbie raised his chin. "I care for Charles."

Charles wondered which of the two cousins, Samuel or Robbie, was the greater fool. "He's never done anything in this hall to shame you," Charles said, dismissing their furtive kisses and embraces.

Honestly, this was all one person's fault. He turned to study the guilty party. "Samuel, you're a malicious sort of a brat, aren't you."

"You come into my house, misuse my hospitality, abuse my nephew and then think you have the right to malign my son?" Phillip's voice was too high and tight.

"He did not abuse me," Robbie said.

"Perfect Robbie is a pervert, Father," Samuel said.

Charles really had had enough of him. He walked over with only the slightest limp now, drew back his fist and hit Samuel. He checked the blow—he'd boxed a little at university and knew how to put his full strength behind a punch. This was an openhanded, nearly genteel slap, but Samuel stumbled, then howled as if he'd been laid out and pummeled.

A moment later, Phillip had called for Stewart, and Charles was being hauled back to a chair and pushed down into it. Robbie protested, Samuel cursed and Phillip shouted.

Charles closed his eyes and wished he hadn't indulged in the urge to hit Samuel, or perhaps he should have punched his fist into him a little harder.

The door to the office opened and slammed shut.

"What is going on in here?" Lenore demanded. "Samuel, your awful friend Jarrod Watersmith insists you have some sort of appointment with him, and he won't go until you talk with him. I came to find you, and I could hear the noise from down the stairs and..."

She stopped speaking for a moment, then said, "Ah. You may go, Stewart, thank you for all of your work tonight." Lenore waited until the footman left the room to continue. "It sounded as if you were having a brawl. In our house. Samuel, why is your cheek red?"

Samuel pointed at Charles. "He hit me."

Lenore crossed her arms over her bosom and glared at them all, one by one. Charles was surprised he didn't get even the lion's share of her disgust. She saved that for her son. "I was going to send you to speak to your friend, but that is a distinct pattern of a hand on your cheek, and that won't do. Robbie, please, perhaps you should go pay off Watersmith, since I'm sure that's what he wants. Yes, don't adopt that confused look, Samuel. I know about your gambling."

Robbie rose to his feet slowly. "Certainly. The man's still here, then?"

"If we give him fifty pounds, he'll go away for now," Samuel said. He gave a long sniff and rubbed at his pink cheek.

"I will attend to it. None of you move." Phillip opened a desk drawer and grabbed a leather purse. He paused at his wife's side and gave her a wan smile. "Of course I was not speaking to you, my dear. Please get back to our guests. I am so sorry." He walked out of the room quickly, pulling the door shut hard behind him.

"Why would he say that he's sorry? Except for your nonsense, Samuel, the ball went extremely well. Everyone told me again and again how lovely the decorations are." She sighed. "Of course we shall have to cope with your foolishness. Oh, why did you behave so badly? During my ball too? You know how much I look forward to this." She sounded her usual querulous self, which made Charles feel much better.

"I had to, Mother. I was trapped."

She only shook her head. "And look how upset your father is."

"Oh, that wasn't because of me. Not at all."

Charles moved over to Samuel and muttered, "Are you sure you want to talk about this? With your mother?"

But of course he did. Anything to wiggle out from under the weight of his mother's disapproval. "I hardly like to tell you, Mother, but my father's angry and upset about Robbie."

"What? Why?"

Now Samuel looked uncomfortable. "Because of Robbie and Charles. They are... They have... They have an unnatural relationship. It's disgusting."

"What does that have to do with my ball being ruined with your thievery? And what do you mean? No, no, I beg of you, don't tell me. I know they are good friends."

"*More* than good friends."

"Samuel, would you stop talking nonsense," she snapped. "I'm sure that Robbie has been far more cheerful since Charles has come to our house, and we all can see he is a good influence on Charles." She pursed her lips, no doubt remembering his disastrous arrival. "Anyone can see that you're a better man than when you first arrived."

Charles hid a smile. "Thank you, I agree," he said.

"But, Mother, they kiss. Like—like a betrothed couple. And they do other things."

"Samuel, you've been annoying enough this evening. We don't need any more drivel from you. I fear you are drunk. Robbie, do take him to bed."

"I don't need *him* to help me to bed. He might try to do something to me."

"Samuel. Enough! How many times do I have to tell you? Be quiet!" his mother ordered. "You are giving me a headache. Go up to your room. And don't you dare show yourself in company, not with that red mark on your cheek."

He slumped from the room.

Robbie began to speak, "Aunt Lenore, I'm sorry. I have tried to—"

She folded her arms. "I have no interest whatsoever in that nonsense he was discussing. I am sure it is none of my business, and I don't wish to hear another word."

Her gaze went to the door, then down at her purple gown, then she looked at Robbie. "What people do or don't do is no one's business. I find the subject utterly distasteful. You and Charles are obviously good companions, and more than that I do not wish to hear."

Robbie ducked his head. "But I—"

"I am not interested." For a moment, her mouth twisted into a sneer, or perhaps a smile. "If I should ever attempt to describe what happens when a husband and wife are alone, I beg of you to send me to a madhouse."

She reached up with one gloved hand and touched a feather on the elaborate display of jewels, beads and feathers on her head. "This confection you designed for me received so many compliments tonight, I cannot begin to tell you, but I think it's adding to my headache. I would like to go to bed as soon as possible. I can't, of course, not until the last guest leaves or retires." She heaved a sigh. "And all this business of Samuel sneaking about... It's in such terrible taste. I suppose I should return to our guests."

"Have a cup of tea first," Robbie suggested.

"I'd love that, darling Robbie, but it will have to wait." Her nostrils flared as she stifled a yawn. Charles felt the urge to yawn too. All of the *Sturm und Drang* seemed to be concluded for now, the storm quenched by the rather inane Lenore, although that was his old opinion of her. Now he couldn't help thinking that she was most sensible of the Chester lot, followed by Gemma.

They paused before heading back to the ball and shouldn't have, because a moment later, Phillip came into the room. He slammed the door behind himself and slapped the purse onto the desk. The way he folded his arms looked very much like his wife's indignant posture. He echoed her with the words, "As if I already didn't have enough on my plate. You two gentlemen"—and the way he drawled that word said volumes—"are now polluting my home. That problem, at least, I can easily dispose of."

Charles looked at the pale Robbie and wished he could go mutter something encouraging to him. Something cheery like *buck up* or perhaps a filthy joke would do the trick.

Lenore's voice was shrill. "Phillip, don't you start with the disgusting insinuations, or I shall scream. I promise you, I will."

Phillip stammered, "Oh. Ah. My dear, I didn't see you. That is, I thought you would have gone to our, ah, other guests. There are still a few guests here, and I think you should attend to them at once."

"I was about to do just that. Robbie, Charles, if you would please escort me back to the ballroom. I'm sure the way the family abandoned our guests is most peculiar. Do get your cane, Robbie. Your leg must be bad tonight."

"They will not go among our guests," Phillip began.

"I was entirely serious when I said I would scream," Lenore said in a loud, quavering voice. "Charles and Robbie are the only men in this family who have behaved with any decorum tonight. The way they came to my aid with the sisters should earn them a medal—oh Lord, Phillip get out of my way. I *shall* scream when I think of my son."

She wrenched open the door in a most unladylike manner and stormed out of the room. The silence after her exit was sudden and absolute for a full minute, only the distant sounds of the orchestra disturbing it.

Phillip exhaled audibly and rubbed a hand over his face before finally speaking, and he continued to look at the surface of his desk rather than at either Charles or Robbie. "I do not pretend to understand your behavior, how it is even possible for—" He raised a hand, cutting off the thought. "But it doesn't matter. This is what will happen next. You will both pack all your things and leave here tomorrow. There will be a train to the city in the afternoon. You will be on it."

"Yes, sir," Robbie murmured.

Charles looked over at his friend's lowered face and chastened expression. His heart ached at the sadness in his gray eyes. He would do anything to alleviate it. "Please, Cousin, don't punish Robert for this. If you cut him off, send him away without a reference or financial assistance after all he's done for you, now *that* would be a crime."

Phillip glared at Charles at last, his eyes on fire. "Don't presume to tell me how to deal with my nephew, *Cousin.* I do not forget Robbie's years as a member of this family, nor would I destroy him due to behavior I believe was brought on by your tainted presence. I will make his introduction to several of my friends in the city as promised. A position at one of their companies will provide him with future security."

He turned his attention to Robbie, and a look of such heartbreak contorted Phillip's face that Charles nearly felt sorry for him. "You have been as a son to me these many years, and so I will continue to watch over you as a father would any son. I would not see you continue down this road to ruination. My agent in the city will help you find suitable lodgings. For *one,* is that understood? Any further friendship between the two of you must cease. If I learn Charles has been a visitor to your rooms, I will withdraw my support."

Phillip drew a breath, and Charles almost rushed in to fill the pause with protests. He wished Robbie would do it, speak up for himself, insist that he would live his life however he damn well pleased. But Robbie spoke not a word.

"Because your Aunt Lenore and the younger children love you so dearly, I will not banish you forever from our home. You may return for holidays and occasional visits. But again, if I learn of *any* interaction between you and this man, or any other man, my offer is rescinded. Is that clear?"

Robbie lifted his chin at last and gazed directly into Phillip's eyes. "Yes, Uncle, I understand. What about Charles?"

"I will give him assistance too while he finds employment, although I can't imagine any position you're suited for." He directed his angry glare back at Charles. "Now, I am very tired and have nothing more to say. Both of you may go."

The old Charles would have had so much to say. In his pride and arrogance, he would never have allowed anyone to speak to him in such a manner. But the new Charles recognized that, as much as it galled, he was greatly beholden to a relative whom he had deeply wounded. Further words right now would benefit no one. He dug the tip of his cane into the carpet and dragged his weary bones upright.

Robbie did the same. He spared Charles not so much as a glance before leaving the room. The ache inside Charles deepened as he watched his lover walk away from him. The symbolism of that exit was not lost on him, and he felt as if a chasm had opened between them, some great ravine without a bridge to cross it. Those ephemeral moments with Robbie were over, and a long, lonely road stretched before him.

Chapter Eighteen

When changes happen in life, they often rush at one quickly and unexpectedly, Robbie mused as he removed shirts from his wardrobe and packed them in his trunk brought down from the attic. Sometimes those changes rode in on a carriage, drunk and loud and overbearing. Other times they took the form of a quiet voice delivering an ultimatum and ending a lifelong relationship. Even if he came to the hall at Christmases to see Gemma, Bertie and Lenore, Robbie realized his uncle considered him as good as dead. That fatherly presence he'd so admired and loved over the years no longer cherished him in return. The abrupt loss hit him like a blow to the stomach, and, although none of it was Charles's fault, Robbie couldn't deny his anger at Charles for instigating the changes which had led to this. True, with Samuel's return, Robbie would have left eventually, but not under a cloud of darkness and humiliation, and with his uncle's condemnation ringing in his ears.

He jammed the shirts down deep into the chest to make room for trousers and tried to imagine himself wearing these clothes in some other life, perhaps working as an accountant in a dreary, windowless office. Robbie recognized his glorious indulgence in self-pity for what it was, but that didn't stop him from feeling it. Probably he should have forced himself to get some sleep instead of immediately starting to pack in the middle of the night. He was too tired, that was his problem. The wave of anger at Charles had passed, and he knew he could never hate Charles. In fact, he wished he dared go to the room so close to his and see the man who had changed his life, but under the present circumstances, it wasn't wise.

Anyway, they would have the entire train ride to London during which to talk and plan some sort of future together. For, despite Phillip's conditions, Robbie knew he *would* find a way to be with Charles. Even at the risk of destroying his relationship with the rest of his family, that was a given. For better or for worse, as the sacred vow went, he and Charles were now a pair.

By the time Robbie had packed away the last of his possessions—which included boxing every reminder that he'd ever lived in this house to be stored in the attic or perhaps burned with the rubbish—morning light shone into his room. He went to the window to gaze at the sunrise, perhaps his last under this roof. His room, his home no longer.

Robbie washed up and put on fresh clothes for the new day, the day he would travel by train to an uncertain future. Suddenly, instead of making him feel a bit queasy, he was filled with excitement at the prospect. A bright morning could lift one's spirits, making anything seem possible.

He gathered up the keepsakes he'd saved for Bertie and Gemma. He had a slingshot for Bertie, which the boy had always coveted. It had been Robbie's as a lad. He hadn't given it to his cousin before now because he'd doubted the boy's responsibility in using the weapon. A little chat about not harming animals would be in order before he surrendered the slingshot into Bertie's possession.

His other gift was for his darling Gemma. She was too young to care about it now, but might someday, as a remembrance of the cousin who loved her. And, just in case the gift of his sketchbook and drawing implements might prove disappointing to a small child, Robbie also added a book of fairy tales with colored illustrations, which he'd purchased for the upcoming Christmas. Let her enjoy it early. He would buy something else for her later, although he may have to send it by post if he was banned from the house for the holidays.

With his presents in hand, Robbie started up toward the nursery to find the little girl he knew would already be awake and having breakfast with Nurse Mary. But when he arrived, the large room was empty. A peek into Gemma's small bedroom showed the messy and empty bed. A chill of unease swept through him as he walked through the vacant rooms. The hairs on his neck prickled, warning that something was wrong here, and when he came out into the hallway, Mary's frantic arrival proved his suspicion true.

She practically flew up to him, her hair straggling from under her cap, her eyes wide and her face red. "Is she there? Has Gemma returned? Oh please, Mr. Robert, say that you took her for an early morning walk and have brought her back."

"Gemma is missing? She's probably out in the stable with her dogs or perhaps playing hide-and-seek with you. I shouldn't worry too much, Mary." But his nagging sense of unease grew.

Mary forgot her place and snapped at him. "Of course I checked all her usual spots. You may believe I let her run wild, but I'm not a fool. I know my little girl. I've had all the staff combing the house for her, and she's nowhere to be found. Nowhere!"

Robbie racked his brain. "You know how excited she was by the ball and the houseguests. Maybe she slipped into one of the guest's rooms and fell asleep underneath a bed or in a closet." This large dwelling had a lot of nooks and crannies.

Mary threw up her hands. "What am I to do? I can hardly go door to door, waking the guests and asking if anyone's seen Gemma."

"It's too soon to raise a search party. She might pop up at any moment," Robbie said. "Did you check the garden? You know she's made herself a little house underneath the branches of the weeping cherry."

"Yes. We've scoured the garden and all the outbuildings." Mary paused, and a new frown creased her forehead. "Would she have dared go beyond the yard?"

"Possibly." Robbie led the way downstairs with Mary treading heavily behind him. "You haven't informed the Chesters yet?"

"No," Mary panted. "Not until I'm certain there's a need to worry."

"And how long ago did you discover her missing?"

"First thing this morning. She wasn't in her bed. It was about six o'clock. Miss Gemma rises early, the sweet little thing, always so happy to greet the n-new d-day." Muffled sobs came from behind him. "None of our guests are awake yet, say the maids, but should we go door to door?"

"Now, now, Mary. This is no time to lose composure. Nothing has happened to Gemma. She will turn up shortly." Robbie spoke calmly, as much to reassure himself as to comfort her. But it was nearly eight o'clock. For always hungry Gemma not to show up for breakfast was worrisome.

Robbie and Mary took the servants' staircase. He had no desire to run across either Lenore or Phillip, although likely after the night's exhausting events they'd still be abed. For Mary's sake, it was better to resolve this situation without involving the family.

In the servants' dining hall off the kitchen, Robbie conferred with the butler, Mr. Falston, and Mrs. Jackson, the housekeeper. Several maids and footmen lingered nearby, eager to be involved in the morning's excitement.

"Stewart." Falston summoned the footman from lurking. "You checked the stables? No one saw Miss Gemma there playing with her wee doggies?"

"No, sir."

"Could she have curled up in one of the carriages, fallen asleep and traveled home unnoticed with one of our guests?" Mrs. Jackson suggested. "With young Gemma, all things are possible."

A clamor of possibilities arose as every member of the staff, down to the scullery maid, had some insight to offer. At last Robbie raised a hand to silence them.

"To start with, I will get Daisy. Likely the dog will lead us to Gemma, wherever she is."

"Unless she's indoors," Rose, the second maid, muttered, and Mr. Falston quelled her with a look.

Robbie went to put on his coat and hat and headed across the yard toward the stables. He was nearly there when a familiar voice called after him, "Robbie. Wait."

He glanced back to see Charles moving toward him with an ungainly stride, a bit like a sailor used to the pitching deck of a ship. Robbie waited for him to draw closer, then called out, "Gemma's missing. More than usual. The servants and I are searching for her."

"Let me help." Charles strode a little faster. "Perhaps Daisy can track her down."

"That's why I'm going to the stables. If you want to help, I'd appreciate it if you'd take charge of things in the house. She could well be there or in the gardens. Lenore and Phillip will soon be up, as well as the houseguests. I don't wish to alarm them prematurely, but at some point, we may need to organize a search party."

Charles frowned. "You think it might come to that?"

"I don't know." Robbie had been feigning confidence for Mary's sake, but now his creeping sense of anxiety resurfaced. "I feel as if something may be wrong."

Charles nodded curtly. "All right, then. I'll handle things at the house, and you search with the dog."

For one more moment, they stood looking at each other. Charles's hair blazed like copper in the bright sunlight. His brown eyes were fierce and his handsome jaw set. He opened his mouth as if to add something, then closed it again, nodded and turned to walk back to the house.

Robbie went into the cool darkness of the stable, where horses chuffed quietly in greeting from their stalls. The earthy scents of hay and dung enveloped him. He called out, and Forrester came from the rear of the building.

"Has Miss Gemma turned up yet?" Extra seams of worry carved Forrester's already wrinkled brow. He stroked his tobacco-stained moustache in a habitual gesture.

"No. And you're sure she wasn't here to visit with the dogs this morning?"

"No one saw her. Dickie. John," he called and the stable hands appeared like summoned genies. Both hands confirmed that they hadn't laid eyes on the child.

The trio accompanied Robbie out to the kennels behind the stable, where hunting hounds used to be kept. Since the current Mr. Chester wasn't a hunting man, several mixed-breed mutts now occupied the runs.

Robbie counted five, including the bitch which had whelped Daisy and a couple of her progeny. The rest of the pups had gone to new homes. Robbie moved close to the fence and reviewed the pack again. Daisy was not among them.

"She's taken her dog out. You didn't notice?" he demanded. Then he remembered the scene when Lenore had banished the dog from the house. Perhaps Gemma had gone out to rescue the dog and had taken it for a walk.

"Uh." Dickie scratched his head.

Robbie exhaled a breath and tried to release his anger at their stupidity along with it. "This means she's someplace outside, or someone would have heard that dog by now." He looked across the pasture to the woods beyond. "I think it's time to organize the staff and expand the search."

One couldn't call upon the entire staff to abandon their posts and begin searching for a missing child without the lady of the house noticing that something was amiss, especially when a half dozen guests had been awakened to have their rooms searched as well. After Robbie informed him of the progression in the situation, Charles took it upon himself to find Lenore and tell her of Gemma's disappearance. She flew into a panic and nearly required smelling salts to revive her as she swooned.

Charles guided her into a chair. If she bore any ill will toward him or, indeed, any memory of the previous night's drama, Lenore addressed Charles as she normally would.

"Have they checked the attic? Gemma loves to explore."

"The attic, the cellar and every place in between," Charles assured her. "It's become quite clear that Gemma isn't in the house or the gardens. The fact that she's probably taken her dog suggests she's gone someplace farther afield than normal. The woods are the most likely place, since she's expressed great interest in the games Bertie and his friend play there."

Click. A simple, obvious thought dropped into place in his mind. "Bertie's fort! That's where she's trying to go."

He squatted beside Lenore's chair. "I think we can't keep this news from Phillip or the company. It would be best to let everyone know. Shall I inform them for you?"

Lenore fluttered the handkerchief she'd been wiping her eyes with. "Yes, please. I'm...distraught. I hardly know what to do."

So much for the temporarily forceful woman who'd shown herself last night, Charles thought. He hurried toward Phillip's office, his leg seeming to ache more with every step since it was the last place in the world he wanted to go. He knocked, then went inside.

As expected, Phillip and Samuel were in conference. Mr. Todd was not present. Both father and son looked up upon Charles's entry and he was struck by the similarity in their appearance, two blond, blue-eyed Chesters with nearly three decades difference between them. Charles felt he could see what kept them apart, besides the obvious fact of Samuel's irresponsibility. Phillip had forgotten what it was like to be so young, and Samuel couldn't begin to imagine being so old. They had no common ground.

"May I help you?" Phillip asked coolly. "Are you ready to leave for the station?"

Charles almost smiled. It was midmorning, and the next train wouldn't leave until late afternoon. Phillip couldn't wait to see the back of him. "No. I've come to tell you something. About Gemma." He paused, searching for better words, but there was no good way to break such news. "She's gone missing this morning, and it's become clear she's nowhere in the house or on the grounds. The servants are organizing to search the woods."

Phillip rose. "What? My daughter is missing and I'm the last to be told?"

"Gemma has a habit of playing hide-and-seek," Charles soothed him. "Until everyone was certain she was truly gone, there seemed to be no point in worrying you."

"Lord, but she's a little scamp," Samuel said. "And Mary is useless with her. She's too old and fat to be looking after children any longer."

She's not that old, and Gemma is exceptionally active for a girl. Charles found himself wanting to defend the servant, but he bit back the words. "It's occurred to me that she's trying to find Bert's fort. If he could lead us there, it might be a good beginning point."

Samuel stood by his father's side. "I'll find her, Father. She's my sister. We don't need these outsiders directing us on what to do. And neither one of them could walk in the woods anyway."

The little blighter had a point. Neither Charles nor Robbie would be of much use tripping over roots and logs and uneven ground when they could barely walk straight on smooth floors. Being a part of the search was clearly not possible for either of them.

But not forever, Charles thought. His legs grew stronger every day, the broken bones healing. And he hadn't felt any sign of the weird tingling disease with its attendant loss of control for weeks now. One day this entire episode of his life would be nothing but a bad memory, except, of course, those parts with Robbie.

"Robbie and I will stay at the house, then, and look after Cousin Lenore and tend to the guests," he declared, staring at Samuel and daring him to defy him on this.

"Very well." Phillip closed and locked his desk before leading the way from his office. "Let us go find your sister."

As it turned out, several of the guests insisted on joining in the search, while their wives rallied around Lenore, offering sympathy and support. There was little for either Charles or Robbie to do except search the garden one more time. After much walking and calling, they returned to Lenore's sitting room to report to her and the ladies.

"One more search around the house," Charles declared.

"From the attics to the cellar," Robbie said.

"Yes, do go once more." Lenore sniffed and waved her handkerchief at them as if they were about to head off on a journey. "Thank you, my darlings."

"I might not be able to gallop around the countryside yet, but waiting for word and doing nothing is intolerable. If I'd stay in this house, inactive, I will start swinging from the chandelier like a gibbon monkey," Charles said as they started their slow walk up to the attic.

In the dusty attic, they opened trunks and poked through wardrobes.

Charles hesitated when they arrived at the servants' quarters. "This seems intrusive," he pointed out. "And they've already searched their own rooms."

"Yes, but if she's hiding somewhere inside, she might have moved about the house since then."

"All right," Charles agreed.

The search through those rooms revealed nothing—except the fact that Mrs. Jackson didn't keep her small room as neat as the rest of the house and one of the two footmen sharing a room owned three brands of hair oil. They called her name every few seconds.

As they made their slow way down the back stairs, Charles asked, "Are you packed?" And then in a low voice, he added, "I have wanted to say this since last night. I am so sorry for my part in ruining your relationship with your family."

"Your family too." Robbie stopped for a moment and leaned against the wooden handrail. "In the end, I don't believe the truth can be denied. At some point, we would have revealed our—our..." His voice trailed off.

"Affection," Charles finished with a flash of a smile. He turned and continued down the stairs.

Affection, Robbie thought. Exactly that.

"I wish we could return to a time when fear of discovery was our greatest worry," he muttered.

"We'll find Gemma," Charles said without turning around. His hearing and understanding were far too acute.

They had made their way down to the kitchen when Robbie heard something scratching. He put a hand on Charles's arm. "What's that?"

"What do you mean? Oh! That sound."

Robbie moved quickly past him, skirting the huge table and the low-hanging herbs to go through the scullery to the door. He opened it to find a muddy, happy dog sat staring up at him.

"Daisy!"

She bounded into the house, ears flapping, leaving a trail of dirty paw prints. She sniffed around the kitchen with that eager excitement of a young creature invading forbidden territory. She stopped at the larder door and, with both front paws, scratched enthusiastically at the spot where the door and flagstones met.

Robbie watched, dismayed. "Daisy, we're not going to feed you, you awful animal. Find Gemma. *Gemma.*"

Charles opened the door and peered inside. "Gemma's not in there. Should I fetch Daisy some scraps? Or shall we just shove her back outside and see if she leads us to Gemma?"

"I suspect that if she eats, she will lie down in a corner and go to sleep."

They stared at the panting dog that watched them expectantly.

"She looks almost intelligent," Charles said hopefully.

"Find Gemma," Robbie ordered again. The dog scratched at the larder again.

"All this food is too distracting," Charles declared. He pushed and pulled the reluctant dog back out the kitchen door, into the garden.

Robbie said, "Should we tell someone Daisy has returned?"

"There's no point. She might be useless... Wait, maybe..." Charles pointed at a patch near the kitchen door, not far from the chicken coop. "I see a paw print there. Come on, Daisy, let's follow your trail."

She was perfectly glad to sniff in the vicinity of the coop.

As she sniffed, Charles cursed her, repeating "Find Gemma" a few times for good measure.

Robbie examined the ground carefully. "Perhaps Daisy came from that direction?" He pointed toward the rougher, taller grass, which was more than an inch or so tall and might have been trampled lately. Thank goodness the gardeners hadn't been back there with their clippers.

"You have a good eye, I hope." Charles pushed the sniffing dog in that direction. "Go on. Gemma. Get Gemma," he said.

They watched the circling dog for several long minutes. She lay down and rolled in something, no doubt a bit of rancid chicken droppings.

A few moments later, she led them to a pile of rubbish the gardeners had collected to burn.

"That is the most worthless cur it's ever been my misfortune to meet," Charles said. Robbie agreed. He felt ready to strangle the happy, aimless Daisy.

She stopped sniffing, lifted her head, and her ears pricked forward. One paw rose as she sampled the air.

"Now. She will at last make a move," Charles said, and a moment later, she bounded off into the woods.

The groundskeepers kept the woods clear of underbrush, but Robbie still felt awkward, nearly unbalancing with every step as he crashed after the dog through the woods, stumbling on every root and uneven rise of ground.

Charles took up the rear not making as much noise as Robbie but making up for it by calling "Gemma, Gemma," every few seconds.

Daisy uncovered a pheasant and took off yapping after the flapping bird. They caught up with the dog when she stopped to tree a squirrel and bark at it.

"You must show us Gemma," Robbie ordered.

"Come on, you wretched animal. Leave off," Charles said in the same instant. Their eyes met, and Charles snorted. "If one weren't so worried about Gemma, this would be quite a comic turn, two full-grown men hobbling in giant circles after a stupid dog as she sniffs after every small animal in the woods."

"We'll be able to have a good laugh later, I pray," Robbie agreed absently. Leaves and dirt flew as Daisy dug a hole. "She's apparently found a mole. Do you think we ought to give up and drag her back?"

Another thought seized him. "The lake. Dear God, it's too cold to swim, but Daisy might have gone in. She's so muddy. And then Gemma..." He couldn't finish the sentence.

"No," Charles said roughly. "See how muddy that hole she made is? That's why the bloody animal is wet. Come on, Robbie. We'll follow her another few minutes and then return home."

"Or go to the lake," Robbie murmured.

Charles didn't answer.

The dog abandoned digging and started to trot through the woods. She actually stopped and looked over her shoulder at them.

"I do hope that glance of hers means 'come along, you hobbling, slow fools' and not 'why are you following me?'" Charles said as he began to run again.

They might have missed Gemma if she'd been wearing a different color. First Robbie saw a flash of vivid pink lying on the ground. And then he saw the sprawled child.

For a far too long, terrible moment he thought she was dead and then he saw her chest rise and fall. "There. Thank God," he said and hurried to her.

About a few yards off, Daisy barked up a tree at another squirrel.

Gemma opened her eyes and sat up. "Robbie! I knew you'd find me. Is it too late for breakfast?" She rose to her feet and allowed herself to be seized by Robbie, who'd dropped to his knees next to her.

"You wretched girl," he said, his voice thick. He buried his nose in her damp hair that smelled of dog and woods. "We've been looking and looking for you."

"It's a good thing you put on that coat," Charles said.

Robbie pulled back. He nodded, still stunned by how easily they could have walked past her and not seen her.

Gemma patted her coat. "Robbie doesn't like it. The color is too strong, he said."

"I like it now. I love the beastly thing. You shall always wear bright colors if you insist on wandering from home," Robbie said. Charles walked over and stood by the pair. Robbie allowed himself several seconds of comfort by leaning his back against Charles's legs.

"I didn't insist on wandering. Daisy did." Gemma rubbed her eyes.

Robbie slowly rose to his feet, sliding up Charles's body to steady himself and because he loved having all that grand, solid warmth right there for him.

He held out his hand to Gemma. "Come on, darling. Let's take you home and feed you breakfast."

"Daisy needs breakfast, too, but she got me lost. I wanted to show her the fort, but she would keep making me go in circles."

Robbie said, "The fort? I'd say it's a full mile east of here. The gentlemen have all gone off to search for you in that direction."

Gemma frowned. "They are looking for me? Am I in trouble?"

"You'll get a scolding, I should think," Charles said. "But you'll also get petted and cried over."

Robbie murmured, "I was the first to do that." He surreptitiously wiped the corners of his eyes with his sleeve.

Charles looked around the seemingly endless gray and green haze of the woods. "I have no idea which direction to go. I'm as lost as Gemma."

Robbie pointed. "That way."

Daisy must have noticed they headed back to civilization and food, because she stopped nosing around and took off, heading straight through the woods.

"Now she's running with a single-minded purpose, like a dog with actual brains," Charles grumbled.

"She actually did lead us to Gemma." Robbie smiled down at the girl who held his hand tightly.

"Yes, I suppose it was more than a coincidence," Charles said with some surprise in his voice.

Gemma whined that she was tired. "Carry me, Robbie." She yanked on his hand.

"No, I'm bigger and stronger, so I shall." Charles reached down for her. She went without complaint and clung to him, her arms tight around the neck.

Charles looked at Robbie over her shoulder, first with mock dread, but then he smiled and patted her back.

They walked slowly through the woods, heading back to the packed trunk and the silent disapproval of Uncle Phillip and an uncertain future.

But at the moment, Robbie's relief outshone every other emotion or concern. He walked next to the two people he cared about most in the world and, when Gemma demanded it, he began to sing her favorite nursery song.

"I had a little doggie that used to sit and beg, But Doggie tumbled down the stairs and broke his little leg; Oh, Doggie, I will nurse you, and try to make you well; And you shall have a collar with a pretty little bell. Ah, Doggie, don't you think that you should very faithful be, For having such a loving friend to comfort you as me."

When he paused, Gemma said, "The doggie is just like Charles with the broken leg."

"Yes, and I have the loving friends who'll comfort me—you and Robbie," Charles said.

By the time Robbie and Charles walked out of the woods, all three were singing.

Chapter Nineteen

Aunt Lenore cried. Her friends who'd kept vigil with her wept too. They all hugged Gemma and for many long minutes cooed over her and scolded her as Charles had predicted. Then Mary fetched the girl, promising her an enormous breakfast and a hot bath—and the back of a hairbrush on her bottom should she ever frighten them all like that again.

Aunt Lenore declared that Robbie and Charles were the best, most useful men she knew, and Daisy would be allowed in the house for at least the rest of the day.

By the time the gentlemen had been fetched from their search and returned to the house, the festive atmosphere had settled slightly, but with their arrival, the celebration of Gemma's return began again.

Robbie slipped away up to his room to take one more look around.

As he checked a copy of Bradshaw's to see which trains could take them to London, someone knocked on his bedroom door.

He knew his uncle's sharp tap. "Come in," he said, with some reluctance.

Phillip entered but didn't walk far into the room. He didn't meet Robbie's eyes—instead, he glared at the drapes over the window as if they offended him.

He cleared his throat. "Lenore tells me that you found Gemma."

"Charles and Daisy and I did, yes."

"I thank you for that."

Robbie wished he'd say more, but he only nodded once, then turned away.

"You're welcome," Robbie called after him.

Uncle Phillip turned once again and looked him square in the face. "You are a good and honest person, Robbie. Intelligent too. I shall write a letter to that effect. Lenore says anything else need not be mentioned."

Robbie nodded. He longed to tell Uncle Phillip all of it, the deep affection he held for Charles, the sense of completion he felt near him, the way he felt more alive and funnier and happier and smarter when he was around Charles.

He'd never say any of that to his uncle, or anyone else for that matter—except to the one person who should hear it: Charles.

Soon they would be on a train to London, and he could speak those words, or, if the third-class car was too crowded, write them in a note.

Poor Charles, traveling third class with the livestock. Robbie longed to see him there. But now he must say his good-byes. This moment with Phillip was better than he'd hope for.

His uncle waited, his hand on the door. He seemed to want something else, so Robbie spoke. "Thank you," Robbie said. "For giving me a home and everything else you've done for me. And you've done so very much to help and educate me, Uncle Phillip. Thank you for all of it."

Phillip's mouth twisted. His eyes squinted, he blinked, and for a moment, Robbie wondered if Phillip would allow himself to cry. His own eyes prickled, but he successfully fought back tears.

"I loved you as if you were my own."

Past tense.

"I love you," Robbie said, but didn't rub it in with *and always shall.* He cleared his throat. "I hope you'll allow me to see Gemma again?" He supposed he'd have no better time to ask than after the big rescue in the woods.

His uncle gave a single nod and closed the door behind him, softly at least.

Charles went to say his farewell to Phillip. He found Samuel sitting at his father's large desk, ledger books open in front of him.

Todd, the large and gruff bailiff, stood behind Samuel as if keeping guard. Todd nodded to Charles. "Hear you're leaving, sir."

"Yes, and more to the point, so is Mr. Grayson."

"Now *that* gentleman will be missed, and I don't mind saying so." He glared at the back of Samuel's head. "I'll go fetch myself some tea and be back. And no, Mr. Samuel, I won't add the figures on that ledger. That's your job, sir. I won't be charged with cheating."

Todd strolled from the room.

Samuel hunkered down in the chair and apparently tried to pretend Charles wasn't in the room.

"You achieved your goal of shifting the attention to someone else," Charles said as he settled onto a wooden chair. He was still unsteady enough he wouldn't risk a comfortable, overstuffed armchair.

Samuel mumbled something and rubbed his cheek.

Charles made a guess and said, "Come look me up in London. I'll give you a fair fight then. A good brawl might do wonders for your temperament, you spoiled, ungrateful puppy. Are you even going to say good-bye to your cousin?"

Samuel mumbled again, and this time Charles couldn't understand.

"What?"

"I said my mother will make me. Satisfied?"

"Not really, but unfortunately, dueling is outlawed, and your family would mourn your passing. Just be sure that should you come to London to sow any wild oats, I shall come to hear of it. And I will make sure that Lenore gets that information by the next post." He smiled, thinking of how happy he would be to see some of his more disgraceful friends upon his return. Not exactly a triumphant reentry into society, but he wouldn't have his future any other way.

Charles stood, ready to leave the house as soon as possible. Samuel rested his forehead on his hand and refused to meet his eyes.

"Enjoy your life among the mangel-wurzles," Charles said. Samuel didn't look up, but his shoulders sagged slightly. Good.

Before Charles could escape, Phillip came into the office. He frowned at Samuel and told him to finish his work later. "You will go spend time your mother's friends now, and you will do it politely."

As soon as Samuel left the room, Phillip began with the dire threats centered upon Robbie's well-being and Charles's lax regard. He was speaking of Robbie's intelligence and abilities when Charles interrupted. "If you care for him so much, then tell him so. He values your good opinion far more than he should."

Phillip stopped speaking after that. Charles waited a few seconds, then gave a slight bow and said, "Well, good-bye. I appreciate your generosity when I was so ill."

He turned to leave, but Phillip spoke again. "Wait." He pulled a purse from a drawer—the same one he'd used to pay off Samuel's friends—and flung it at Charles, who stared down at it.

Did he have the dignity to refuse money? No. He'd lost any dignity, real or false, months ago when he'd lost control of his body and finances.

"Thank you," he said as he picked up the leather purse and tucked it away. He took some comfort from the fact that he wasn't so far gone that he stopped to count it in front of Phillip.

"That should pay expenses for at least a few months, if you have finally learned some economy. If you run out of money, do not apply to me for more," Phillip said acidly.

"No, I won't," Charles said. He knew that as soon as he told Robbie about this money, he'd insist they'd have to pay Phillip back, for Charles and Robbie had no intention of staying apart, as Phillip had insisted the previous night. Alas, the troubles that came with a bond connected to an honest man with scruples.

A few minutes later, when he went to take leave of Lenore, she embraced him and slipped another purse into Charles's pocket. She whispered, "If you need funds, write to me directly. I have a great deal of my own, you know. And I know you'll take good care of my Robbie. He's still quite innocent about the city, so you must protect him."

"You should give him the money," Charles said.

"He'd never take it. He's too proud. He is such a dear."

"He is a good man," said Charles, delighted that someone would at last allow him to say nice things about Robbie.

"Indeed he is, and so you keep it. You're more worldly than he."

That was one pleasant way to describe the difference, he thought as he gave her a kiss on the cheek. He fished out some of the coins to tip the servants.

He would miss Lenore and Gemma. And he would even miss Bertie, although somehow the boy had gotten his hands on a slingshot. Charles felt as if he was escaping just in time.

Charles hummed a tune for a long while before he realized it was Gemma's blasted "I Had a Little Doggie" song.

The cart jostled and thumped over every rut as Forrester drove them to the station. The three of them and the luggage were crammed in tight. It seemed fitting to Charles to set off the way he'd arrived, by cart, with Forrester, singing an absurd song.

But now Charles's pockets contained more money than he'd seen in quite some time, a man he held in great affection sat at his side, and he enjoyed better health than he'd had in years. And he was sober as a priest—one who conducted communion with good wine, that was, because, well, he'd had a brandy or two to celebrate Gemma's return. Nearly entirely sober.

He hummed the contagious little ditty, and then next to him, Robbie began to sing the song softly. Forrester joined in. And of course Charles sang too. His head hurt from too little sleep, his leg ached from too much use last night at the ball and today's chase after Daisy. He'd never felt better in his life.

Chapter Twenty

"Madame Girard is our savior!" Charles announced as he banged open the door and entered the three-room flat he shared with Robbie. "She may well supply our bread and butter for the entire year." He inhaled a whiff of beef and pastry that made his stomach rumble, and shouted toward the tiny kitchen, "Are you here?"

"Coming." Robbie entered the living area, wiping his hands on a towel. Charles's already buoyant spirits rose even higher at the sight of the dear man, his wee sleekit mouse with the soft brown hair. Kind, darling Robbit was so easy to love.

"Now what's all this fuss?" Robbie asked, throwing the towel over one shoulder and leaning against the back of one of the two armchairs, the only furnishings they could afford.

"Madame Girard. It appears she may become our mentor. She was taken with your sketches. Declares your style is *tres nouveau* and exciting. She wants you to come see her salon and create a vision *extraordinaire.* Your first real job as a designer! And if others see and love the room, as you know they will, then more work will follow. One day you will be able to cease the dull life of an office drone."

"That sounds all very wonderful, but who exactly is Madame Girard?" Robbie set aside his dish cloth and came to help Charles out of his topcoat.

"An important personage *en la vie bohéme.* A patroness of the arts. Painters, writers, poets, musicians, dancers and more attend her parties. She brings them together with the wealthy but more eccentric members of society, those who appreciate life with a bit more verve and are not afraid to experience new things."

"Ah, I see. She introduces poor artistic types to potential patrons. How very useful." Robbie smiled and walked over to give Charles a light peck on the lips.

"Useful for *us*. I also showed some of my calligraphy. She has many friends who throw soirees and home concerts and other gatherings. They must send invitations, and I will soon be the premiere choice for adding that special touch to their missives."

"You will. I'm certain of it." Robbie's arms went around him and hugged tightly. "And I shall be happy to meet this Girard woman and pray I may develop a design that meets her high expectations. But in the meantime, I won't be quitting my clerking job at Cloverfield and Bay."

"I suppose not. We do need to continue to eat." Charles sighed. "And I will keep working at the stationer's shop while I develop my clientele. The working life can be such a bore. I miss having money. And I must be polite to the most appalling people, poor me."

"Welcome to middle-class life, my poor, impoverished aristocrat," Robbie teased. He took Charles's hand and pulled. "Come. I need to show you something."

Charles followed him to a bedroom so small it only had room for the rather large bed they'd purchased, then struggled to fit through the doorway. They were forced to keep their clothing in a wardrobe in the main living area, which was also where Robbie supposedly slept, if a visitor ever chanced to call. So far, that hadn't been an issue, and the other tenants of this rundown building expressed not the slightest interest in the two men who shared rather tight quarters in flat number four.

"What am I here to see?" Charles asked, searching the room for any sign of change. But there was only the bed with the same beautifully stitched coverlet they'd bought from an old peddler woman with a marketplace stall.

"This." Robbie unbuttoned Charles's waistcoat and pushed it off his shoulders. "And this." He removed his braces, shirt, trousers and smalls piece by piece, leaving Charles standing naked.

Charles shivered both in excitement and because the flat was always a bit chilly. Robbie pulled back the covers on the bed. "Lie down."

"Yes, sir." Charles smiled and did as he was told, but he didn't cover up. Instead, he put his arms behind his head, erection standing at attention, and waited for Robbie to join him.

He watched while Robbie took off his clothing and set it aside. The skinny but leanly muscled body was as familiar to him now as his own. Still, Charles never lost his interest in it. Each time together provided a new exploration, a new perspective of the angles and curves, the satin flesh and coarse hair of his lover's body.

The bed squeaked and sagged as Robbie climbed on. He stooped over Charles and kissed him several times, slow, sensual kisses that woke a hunger in him no beef and pastry could fill. Then Robbie moved down, centering himself between Charles's sprawled legs, and he attended to that eager erection.

Charles relaxed and half closed his eyes, all his excitement over the prospect of a mentor flowing in a new direction. He watched Robbie suck and stroke him with a much more practiced mouth and hand than he'd had when they first met. Wet. Hot. Insistent pulling. And fingers exploring his intimate places.

Charles's hips began to thrust slightly, unable to hold still beneath such ministrations. He groaned and reached down to rest a hand on that bobbing head. Such soft hair ruffling between his fingers. He rocked and moaned and clutched a handful of Robbie's hair, tugging on it now, as the pressure inside him began to build too quickly.

"Stop. Come up here with me," he demanded. "You are too good, and I'll spend before I wish to."

Robbie crawled back up, wiping his mouth on the back of a hand. His gray-green eyes twinkled mischievously. "What would you do now, sir?"

Charles growled and grabbed him and slung him onto his back. "I would have you, balls-deep and rough and fast. What do you think of that?"

"Show me. I'm an eager learner."

Charles obliged. More than obliged. He hurriedly got the ointment they used and applied it liberally to his cock and Robbie's entrance. Then he pushed Robbie's legs up—yes, Robbie's damaged legs could be that flexible when occasion called for it—and he thrust into that wonderful, tight channel with a spearing motion of his cock. The loving finesse he'd used the first few times he'd ever entered Robbie were nowhere to be found tonight. Punishing thrusts that made Robbie cry out and writhe were the order of the evening.

"Do you like it this way?" Charles panted between grunts. "Do you like it rough?"

"Yessss!" Robbie extended the *S* in a sibilant hiss as his body shook beneath Charles's assault. "Harder," he added.

Flesh slapped against flesh, and grunts of exertion filled the small room for the next few minutes. Then the familiar drawing and tightening sensation began, and Charles thrust one final time. He let go, and sweet, sweet ecstasy flowed through him. God, how he loved *possessing* Robbie this way, as if he could keep him so close forever, body to body, heartbeats shared.

Three months they'd lived together now, and he didn't think he could possibly ever tire of being with Robbie, not only in a carnal way, although that was delightful, but sharing their life together in this awful little flat. The place was heaven, and the man he shared it with, an angel.

"Ah," Charles sighed as he withdrew and gently laid Robbie's legs down on the bed. He rubbed them in case they were sore from the unaccustomed strenuous treatment. "All right?" he asked.

"Yes, but..." Robbie indicated his own erection, still full and thick and nearly purple at the head. He was in desperate need of relief.

"My poor Robbit. Allow me to take care of that." Charles descended on him.

Robbie gasped when Charles engulfed his cock. The sensation of being swallowed whole was one he'd grown to crave on an almost daily basis. He spent much of his workdays fantasizing about the time he would have with Charles come evening. He never grew tired of their lovemaking, whether slow and careful or wild and harsh, such as the way Charles had just taken him. And he never grew tired of falling asleep with that warm body curved around his every night.

London, on the other hand, Robbie sometimes tired of. The city was too noisy, smelly, busy and crowded for a man raised on country air, and sometimes he missed the Chesters, particularly Gemma. But overall, he was happy with his new life.

Right now he was very happy with how Charles gripped him and rubbed briskly up and down and the sucking sensation on the sensitive tip of his engorged shaft was... Oh God, it was...

Robbie arched his back, and his hips bucked. He groaned as wave after wave of pleasure washed through him. He hadn't meant to come so quickly. Charles had barely touched him. But Robbie's desire had been building the entire time Charles pumped into him, and the delay of his own gratification caused him to spend too soon.

Charles released Robbie's spent cock from his mouth and chuckled. "A tad eager, my lad."

"Next time will be better." How wonderful that they could do this again in another few hours, after supper perhaps. And again when night fell and they curled up in their bed for the night. Again and again as many times as in as many positions and creative ways as they might invent. Endless possibilities lay before them.

"Eager is good." Charles kissed his cheek and lay beside Robbie, one arm slung over his chest. "I pray you will always be so eager for me."

"And you for me," Robbie murmured. "I worry sometimes, with all the experience you have, that being only with me might seem dull to you."

Charles pushed up on one arm and gazed down into his eyes. "Never, Robbie. Don't ever entertain such a thought again. As you say, I have had experiences, so I know exactly what I'm *not* missing. You are all I want. In fact, if anyone is to worry, it should be me. You haven't had a chance to try on different men. How do you know I am the right one for you?"

Robbie stared back at him, honestly bewildered. "You're *Charles*. Who else could I possibly want? I love you."

"And I you, Robbit. How could I ever imagine that a disease that stole my health and wealth and all earthly possessions from me might bring me to the very best part of my life?"

Robbie smiled. "And how could I guess that the rollicking drunkard who fell on me at our first meeting would become the man I *want* to fall on me repeatedly."

Author's Note

In the story, Charles's mysterious illness remains unnamed because the condition wasn't recognized until decades after *Mending Him* took place. Sufferers were often accused of hysteria, in part because they improved without any sort of outside treatment.

Charles suffered from Guillain-Barré syndrome, named after the French physicians Georges Guillain and Jean Alexandre Barré, who described it in 1916.

GBS is a rare disorder in which the body's immune system attacks its nerves, sometimes after an episode of flu. Weakness and tingling in the extremities are usually among the first symptoms. These sensations can quickly spread, sometimes paralyzing the whole body. Patients usually exhibit their greatest weakness or paralysis days or weeks after the first symptoms occur. The worst symptoms will continue for a period of days, weeks, or, sometimes, months. Full recovery can be slow, sometimes taking a year or longer. About thirty percent of those with Guillain-Barré still have a residual weakness after three years. Over ninety percent eventually recover completely.

About the Authors

To learn more about Bonnie Dee go to http://bonniedee.com. Send an email to Bonnie Dee at bondav40@yahoo.com. Join her Yahoo! group at http://groups.yahoo.com/group/bonniedee.

Her Facebook is http://facebook.com/people/Bonnie-Dee/1352577313 or you can follow her on Twitter: @Bonnie_Dee.

Summer Devon is the alter ego of author Kate Rothwell. To learn more about Kate/Summer, go to http://katerothwell.com or http://summerdevon.com.

She has a blog: http://katerothwell.com and is on Facebook too: https://facebook.com/S.DevonAuthor. Yes, and Twitter as well: @KateRothwell

It's all about the story...

Romance

HORROR

Retro ROMANCE

www.samhainpublishing.com

Made in the USA
San Bernardino, CA
22 March 2016